Other books by Sherrie DeMorrow:

Knight and Daye
Cloud of Dreams
The Elder Rose
All The Land
The Little Bird
Beyond the Land
A Little Princess
Romancing the West
The Silver Millions
The Painted Chapel

THE PAINTED CHAPEL

BY

SHERRIE DEMORROW

Published 2020 by

Lightning Source (UK) Ltd
Chapter House,
Pitfield,
Kiln Farm,
Milton Keynes
MK11 3LW,
UK

Cover Art Design by Sam Wall

To LL for help and support

and

To the memories of DS, WH, WT, LO, JQ,
and especially TO'C,
who inspired this story

PREFACE

Although this could not be mentioned before, please be advised that there are sections of this book, as in the previous books, that contain *actual* life experiences, emotions and memories. In the guise of fiction, it is the only way to inform the public of the results of an extreme lifestyle and treatment toward a helpless child (now fully grown and *still suffering daily, the aftershocks of such treatment*). It is to be further noted that this individual suffers from a spectrum disorder called Asperger's Syndrome, which is a form of Autism. The author hopes this will not affect the enjoyment of the following, as well as the previous stories already written.

Despite the disclaimer in the aforementioned paragraph, please note this is still a book of fiction. The reader must suspend all preconceptions of belief in past history, as this book is not meant as an accurate representation of historical events (except in the case described in previous paragraph).

The historical attitudes towards sensitive issues, and people's prejudices of the time, had to remain intact to provide a sense of realism in the story. No historical figures represented herein had been harmed during the writing of this work.

Some place names given are **NOT** real, unless otherwise stated or recognised as real (or based on real places). Other characters (for the most part) are fictional and loosely based on people known of by the author.

CHAPTER I

The harbour lights of Queens-Cobhayr burned brightly, signalling incoming ships into it. It was a late summer evening in 1391. The sky was a mass of cloud and wind; the two meteorological elements that loved to be together...

... like the two lovers, King Muffyhuer and his Queen, Lowry Cindihan.

I sensed them above and as the legend told, they were the first occupants of the area now known as Oconnalow, Ireland, where I lived. It was a district a few miles away inland, located in the south near Cork. Yet, the story went on to say that not only were they the occupants of the land...

... in an act of love, they *became* the land...

... and unto it, a child called Conna Daye was born...

... from whom I am descended.

My origins, though, were not as spectacular. I was just a farm lad, named Timoseph Wendel Daye. Most people nicknamed me Wendie, despite the feminine sounding vibe. The Dayes went far back into history and very proud of the heritage it brought us...

... especially the sacred rites at Oconnalow, which was a re-enactment of Cindihan and Muffyhuer's *commitment* to each other...

... before their disappearance into the land itself.

My middle name had a curious history, though:

A passing-by Saxon from England called Wendel travelled to Ireland, long ago in the 400s. He came around the time of St Patrick and the banishment of snakes, purportedly to be of the Saint's doing. As Wendel journeyed forth, he ran into this reptilian exodus. Unfortunately for him, a snake had bit him and he collapsed in the roadside. The snake was thus satisfied and carried on leaving, alongside the rest of its peers.

Meantime, Wendel had a vision; whether it was the dazzle from sunlight, or an actual vision of God, one could never guess. He prayed and hoped someone would come along to assist him in his hour of need. He thought he saw someone familiar... St Patrick? It turned out that was not a vision, but the actual fellow himself. Patrick led him to safety to a nearby farmhouse. A woman called Bridget had cared for Wendel and nursed the wound, which eventually healed.

Wendel had realised the miracle, as snake bites were difficult to deal with in those early times. He turned his heart to the Lord and confessed his faith in Christianity. He asked Bridget about contemplation and his wish to change his life around the new religion. She guided him to a local cave and there, he joined a like-minded group, and began anew, with a more satisfying relish...

... and he never returned to England.

He later founded (with a few other colleagues) a local church called St Wilfrid's-of-Hyde, naming it after a friend he left back in England. Wendel served it publicly as a priest, though he preferred the solitary offerings within the walls of the cave he once lived in.

With all the supposed folklore and history floating 'round my head, I passed a gentle gaze toward the expanse of sea. I was proud to belong here, yet I had wondered if there was more to it 'out there'.

The vast world had opened its arms to me, and if my daydreaming wasn't enough to get me exploring, then nothing would...

... for those embers of fire never died.

A voice hurriedly called out my name. 'Wendie!'

I turned around. It was my sister, Jaicyn.

She thus continued, 'Wendie, Mother wants us back home. She's worried about you.'

'Jaice,' I replied, calling her by the nickname, 'I am more than old enough to look after my own being. Mother doesn't have to continue to wipe my ass indefinitely.'

'You know how she fusses over the most trifling things, especially dinner getting cold. Now, come on,' Jaice beckoned.

'She can burn the house down over it, for all I care!'

'Ooooh,' she pouted. 'You men. Well, I'm going. Suit yourself. Go rot y'hide, Mother will just come a-looking.'

'Let her,' I cried loudly, 'She can have my insides to sell at market if she so wishes!'

Jaice walked stoically away from me, heading for home. I knew I was being brash with her, but it only juiced up the rivalry between us. It was fun, and I relished secretly to constantly make merry with her through conflict. I loved her dearly, but I felt she needed to know her place...

... even if she were the eldest child in our family.

I had a final, parting look at the starry sea, when I realised my tummy was as barren as a virgin womb. I did not like being teased by inner discord, and decided to race the ol' girl to the homestead after all. Mother's food had a traditionally cooked sense of 'alright' woven in, so *that* could not be ignored.

Leaving my petty dreams at the dockside, I ran to catch up with Jaice...

... and snuck up from behind. 'Hiya.'

She swerved in surprise. 'Wendie!'

'You didn't think I'd miss out on dinner, did you?'

'With Mother's hours-long preparation, no, you wouldn't. You couldn't. I can see it in you.'

I blushed hard, knowing she was right.

We went home to Oconnalow, hitching up to a wagon rider bringing supplies toward nearby Harris-on-Ford. Our farmhouse was not too much further. It was a typical old-fashioned stone cottage sort. We lived there with our parents, Jaicyn and Ellias Daye. As Mother and my sister had the same name, we started to call my sister Jaice, as to separate the two females in our household...

... I guess it was better than calling her 'Junior'.

My folks were farmers, and we had a good plot to farm from. There were chickens, some cattle and imported pigs from Totteringstate, England.

Ducks came and went, flying around, swimming in the pond, and breeding to high heck. We bought, sold, and traded at the market for new supplies and livestock. The Totteringstate pigs were boasted as the best, and they didn't come cheap...

... so we bought a male and female to liven our farm and tables with...

... and sold them to others to liven *their* farm and tables.

It got pretty lucrative, and our lives were not limited to a peasant-style of existence. We Dayes were not 'of the land' gentry, but we were not 'of the shit' either. We felt we were better than shit. We lived simply; counting the cost of our needs and fulfilling the price for others.

We also adhered devoutly to God and attended Mass every week. St Wilfrid's-of-Hyde was our home parish and all the Dayes grew up there. St Wilfrid's was one of the earliest churches in Oconnalow; a sweet little place painted white, with a button of a steeple on top. It had an elegantly rustic look about it, but by no means was it frumpy. Ornate stained glass windows splashed sunshine inside, illuminating exquisite frescoes on the walls, painted by local artisans. On Sundays, the church bells rang out; the sounds could be heard as far as Cobh's Reach. It was a romanticised moment for all; the comfort they provided more than made up for the meagre existence most townsfolk shared together.

Jaice and I walked into the little farm patch we called home. Mother looked up from setting the table.

'Where've you been?'

'No place and every place, Mother,' I answered, as I kissed her cheek.

'I caught him dreaming at the harbour again,' Jaice snitched.

'So I was dreaming, big deal,' I scoffed.

'Wendie, you should get a trade,' Mother suggested. 'If you're so hung-up on harbour life, then cast your line out as a fisherman, perhaps?'

I groaned at her punning joke...

... but it was no joke to be unemployed.

'I'll think about it,' I said, half-cocked.

'Good. Now wash up,' Mother ordered. 'Dinner will be served shortly.'

Jaice and I went out back to the stand next to the well. I partially filled a bucket that we shared and washed up. I dumped the rest onto the grass that surrounded us.

We returned to eat a sumptuous meal consisting of beef stew and vegetables, accompanied by a hearty pudding and ale.

Father soon turned up, after a day at the races.

Mother asked, 'Who'd you bet on this time?'

'A hound called Piqwitch. He was good. Them folks just shuddered to see him, and I brought home some earnings.'

He put down a £50 bag's worth of coins...

... no small change, either, but it'll do.

'You know, Elli dear, gambling sucks in the long run,' Mother criticised. 'It cannot last forever, you know. Ye got farm work to do.'

Father looked up at the Cross on the wall, then shot back, 'By th'God, that's what the laddies are fer!'

We looked at each other in bewilderment...

... so Father clarified, 'I meant that in a general sense, as in a plural, referring to you folks. I know you's a growing lady, Jaicyn.'

He went up to kiss her atop her head. When he passed me, he gave me a good tussle and rustled my hair a bit.

'I heard youse been hanging around the harbour again, Wendie. Don't you get enough dreaming in your sleep time?'

I felt ashamed, but stood my ground. 'It's too idyllic a place not to notice.'

'True,' Father agreed, 'But ye must work, too.'

I turned in confrontation. 'So why do you gamble?'

'Cos I cannot get work elsewhere without no schooling! Actually, I do right with my earnings, if I get any,' he explained. 'At least I don't go pissing it away at the local, like other common-folk do. Why waste this shit, when you can save it for when y'need it? Sounds of sense, you know.'

I retorted back, 'And what bank do you put it in?'

'Oh, here and there. That's where the livestock's from. Stock up, raise it, kill it, sell it. Yep, that's the cycle of *where-it's-at.*'

I had to admit that Father was a devil of a schemer...

... and a good one too.

Once we finished eating, we settled into front room activities. Usually, it would be finger-work for Mother, like weaving; Jaice played a rudimentary chess game with me or Father. The pieces we used were made up of a mismatched bits we found around the house. Father sometimes was on his own, humming an odd tune to himself, having a good rest, or he held intimate conversations with Mother, despite our presence...

... it was something to get used to, if you lived in a small farmhouse with only one communal room to share.

'Last I heard about a week ago, they're looking to fill some vacancies at the wharf,' Father said to me.

I looked up from the chess game. 'They've probably filled them by now.'

'Stop ya moaning Wendie,' Mother barked in a huff. 'A Daye never gives up. Tomorrow, I want you to go to your dream port and make your life a reality. Find yerself some work.'

I snapped back, 'Why don't you ask Father to work for a living, huh?'

I got up to walk out, when Father grabbed me at the collar...

... this nearly scared me...

... yet, I knew he was right.

'Listen, Timoseph Wendel Daye, I bust my ass out there, thing to get money for this household, see. Fine, I admit it is an oddity on how I do it. I gamble. So what? I ain't gambling my life away. I use it to fund you lot. Let us state for the record that I am one lucky bastard.'

I posted a conjecture. 'What if your luck ran out?'

'No, no, no,' Father stubbornly protested, 'We are Dayes. We are lucky sods. We are Irish, descended from Conna Daye, the fruit from the passions of Muffyhuer and Cindihan, the Legends and Originators of Oconnalow. It is the good and gracious land you see before us... *Oconnalow...*'

... now, I had to wonder...

... who was the real dreamer here???

'Never mind,' I caved in. 'I'll go look for work i'th'morning.'

'Good,' Father smirked, 'Cos the shops and shipping houses are closed for the night.'

Ha-ha.

I stared at him...

... this tall, gangly, greying man...

... who was my Father, Ellias Daye...

... the self-confessed, lucky sod of Oconnalow.

Christ, what an ass head he could be! He was the perfect intermingling of pride and arrogance. *God help us all, and all the Saints within*!

I went to the upper chamber, leaving my big, fat (in the head), glorious family stumped downstairs...

... and it would take a morning to get there anyway.

CHAPTER II

The next day, I got there...

... and, after a hearty breakfast of quartered oat bread, a slap of ham steak and egg, with ale to drink...

... I made my way toward Queens-Cobhayr...

... but this time, it was not to dream.

'And don't be late back,' shouted Mother over her already bubbling cauldron of good-stuff-for-later.

I sighed heavily, already thinking about the glories of home life. I went down Perry Lane, which led to the wharf site. There was a building on the Lane, dedicated to the Mason's Society, it stood proud-forth in its stony white, with interfacing murals depicting builders at work. It stared out righteously, dominating the other fine buildings that were dwarfed in comparison.

A few moments or so on the cobbled, peach coloured stone pathway, I made it. A huge ship was being loaded for its next voyage to Who-Knows-Where. I asked around to see if I could be of any help.

'Go see Mr Tallis, the foreman over there,' came the speedy answer.

I did so and found myself accepted as a hired hand for this task, loading the ship with precious cargo bound for the East. It wasn't difficult to do, yet my strength was sorely tested. I tried to compare the weight of the boxes to that of a woman, such as my sister (being the only example I could think of). The time was drawn out, long and arduous. I worked very hard to earn my keep there.

Many of the other men first saw me as a puny, gangly sort; a smaller and younger version of my father. These fellows all knew him through their mutual interest in games and gambling.

After a couple of hours slogging it out, Mr Tallis came to me. 'That's your lot for today, lad. Here's a little something for your troubles.'

He handed me a small pouch full of hammered coins of varying shapes and values. I put it in my pocket, when I got taken from behind, and hit with a club...

... and from that, I ended up on the ship I'd just loaded!

When I came to, there was a loud scuffling of feet running in haste to prepare for departure and cast off. All I knew was the ship was heading Eastward, but how far East, I could not tell you. It turned out that I had inadvertently joined a most spartan crew, and I reckoned that the lack of fellows meant anyone could be taken aboard the vessel as crewmen.

I went up to someone and asked, 'What about my family? Wouldn't they be worried about me?'

'What about them,' came an unlikely, but expected answer, 'We've got none, don't we fellas?'

Everyone around me laughed at the naïveté and plain-jane ignorance I displayed, decreed wider than a picturesque fresco at St Wilfrid's.

'Don't fret, lad, word'll get out to your people that you've been called aboard the *Rafferty O'Brien*. They'll forget about you in due time,' came another smart-mouthed answer.

Gosh, I thought, as I tried to reckon my way out of this one...

... it was now my time to grow up.

Working aboard an active sailing ship was not quite what my folks had in mind. With respect to getting a job, this had to have been a doozy. Yet, Mother had told me to cast my line out...

... but what I'll catch from all this, nobody knows.

I did menial tasks in a half-hearted fashion. Not that I was mucking around, you see; I laid out enthusiasm just enough to get by...

... unfortunately, my sentiments shone like a lighthouse beacon on the southern coast of Ireland.

'We don't accept cowering nor cowardice on this ship,' a gap-toothed man said to me.

He smiled at me...

... and I got scared, but held my head up about it.

'I know you're wet behind the ears, but don't get them too wet, lest we throw you overboard,' the man continued.

I checked my ears; they felt dry as a bone. I sweated a little elsewhere, around my body, but I cared not to show it.

I boned up some confidence and introduced myself. 'I'm Timoseph Wendel Daye.'

'I'm Sandy Quade. Sandy is short for Saunder.'

'Call me Wendie.'

We shook hands.

'Good to meet you. It's nice to know I'm not the only one with a girl-bloused name.'

I hung around Sandy for most of the time, now that I've met his acquaintance. Coming from a small district, I found it difficult to get on with others, except for family, naturally. Meeting the other fellows would be another story...

... at least Sandy and I had our effeminate names in common.

Sandy was tall, bulky, muscular, and slanty eyed. He wasn't from the distant East, but his eyes had a slight look of that about them. His physique appeared always prepared for sailing work, and it showed. Ship life wasn't as glamorous as I'd hoped it be. It was harder than I thought. I spent many an hour with him, helping with rigging, mending a sail or two, or cleaning the deck. We worked our hide off; if we didn't, we'd lose some of it with a good flogging.

Of all those aboard the *Rafferty O'Brien*, Sandy was the most hospitable toward me. No one expected life-on-ship to be a social calling. It was either hard work or hard punishment; sometimes forced, other times volunteered. My father's love of gaming and gambling was bountifully shared among the like-minded men, who whiled away their off-duty hours in card games or arm wrestling. However, some of them would rather be dozing off in their hammocks.

Sandy and I engaged in chattering our time away. 'You're not used to ship life, are ye, Wendie?'

'I've worked on my family's farm, thinking it would prepare me for living. It turned out to be more than its nature revealed.'

'Would you leave us?'

I paused, hating the awkward question posed to me. 'If there was something better out there, I probably would. But, as you are my friend, I'll nay forget ye.'

'That's it, my laddie.' Sandy's bear-sized arms embraced me in a firm hug. 'If you're looking for something extra, you could always go to school.'

'School,' I gasped. 'Ain't I a bit too old fer that?'

'Nah, anyone can join in. It's optional at our age,' he sniggered.

'I thought this ship's a classroom and a half!'

'There's more to life than ships. There are the finer things, too... and of course, women.'

My heart pounded at Sandy's mention of the all-hallowed-topic...

... which he noticed immediately. 'Easy, lad. You'll get yer turn. Got to find one first. We're heading East, and there's a port in Italy you can get off at, called Sanbrisi. I believe there's an art school there; it might help you grow up some.'

I blurted out, 'Me, an artisan?'

'Sure, why not. Take up a trade, you know. I can sense you're the romantic dreamer type anyway. You're not fit to work long term on a ship. Yer eyes are shiftin' when I sees ye work.'

Was I that obvious?

Sandy continued, 'I've got a friend at the port who is known as the Hopping Drake, but his name's William Paul. Tell him I sent ye, he'll understand.'

Good God, I blushed... *why was this fella so nice to me???*

I enquired, 'Why's he called the Hopping Drake?'

'He had a childhood accident that rendered a damaged foot, and he cares nought about it, just like a duck's attitude in the rain.'

'Ah, I see. Thank you.' I reflected, realising a good opportunity...

... and I further realised that I would not be home for tea after all.

CHAPTER III

The next several weeks had been quiet and dim among the crew. No one made fusses or whined endlessly over the workload. Everyone got on with their daily business, as did I, just to keep the ship moving...

... and it wasn't long before we reached that Italian port town of Sanbrisi, where an art school awaited a new hopeful pupil that was me...

... yet, judging from the presentation of locality, I knew I wasn't in Oconnalow anymore...

... with no clicking pair of shoes to aid in my escape, if things went hairy on me.

It was a real, live cacophonous din, heard and felt all around me. As cargo was being unloaded, I snuck a quick goodbye to Sandy.

'Too bad ye cannot join me,' I said, 'You've been a good friend.'

'Thank you, lad. It's been my pleasure to help you. I'm too old and stuck in the mud for mad adventures, but you aren't, so get going.'

I gave him a hug, and left him to his heavy cargo.

I looked around like a lost lamb, trying to find a snippet of a tongue I could understand. It was bustling and manic as a market day, but there were no selling stalls set up at port. Business transactions were done on the fly, or on the nail. Whose nail it was, I could not say which. The feeling of being caught up in such a whirlwind was a bit too much. I didn't know if I should cry out for attention, just for the sake of getting assistance; embarrassment was getting the better of me, and there could be bad people about...

... so I had to play my cards right.

The casual 'excuse me' made a ready home on my lips, with its fires burning with curiosity. Finally, in a secluded corner, a familiar speech crossed the threshold of comprehension...

...so, I approached boldly to the gentlemen already in conversation with his partner.

'Hello,' I said.

A moment later, the fellow turned to me to return the call. 'Hello to you. This is my partner, Hamilton Tallis. I'm William Paul.'

'The Hopping Drake?'

'The very same,' he smiled.

'I know a Tallis who's a foreman back in Queens-Cobhayr.'

Tallis smiled. 'That's my twin brother William. I'm business partners with Drake, here.'

I nodded, 'I'm Timoseph Wendel, but you can call me Wendie. Sandy Quade sent me to you.'

Drake recognised his colleague of the sea. 'Ol' Slanty Eyes?'

'That's him,' I smiled. 'I've worked with him aboard the *Rafferty O'Brien*. They just docked to unload some cargo, then they're headed East.'

'Yes, there are spices in the Orient we use here in Italy. We also handle silks, dyes, jewels of all sorts,' Tallis explained. 'Where did you originate from, son?'

'Oconnalow, sir.'

'Ah, so you're Irish,' Drake confirmed.

'Through and through, and proud of it. I am descended from the founders of Oconnalow.'

'You're a Daye?'

'Yep. Wendel's my second name,' I said.

'I never thought I would cruise close to someone so illustrious,' Drake swooned.

'Nah, we're just farmers. It's not like we own the district. It belongs to everybody, just as the founding King and Queen wanted it. They became the land, and there's no trace of them still.'

'Except in you,' Tallis replied, 'Cos from what I heard about the legend, there was a baby found in the vicinity.'

'Yep, that's Conna Daye, my ancestor,' I stated.

'Well, I'm not so grand,' Drake sighed. 'I'm from DeWolfenburg, Germany, born on the Dellastrausse. Tallis is from nearby Hamilburg.'

'You two understand me pretty well.'

'Takes a lot of knowing and hopping about with others to get to know them, son,' Drake said.

'Your duck-like attitude is becoming,' I noted.

'You said it,' he answered.

Tallis asked me, 'So what brings you out, henceforth?'

'I was interested in some art school Sandy was telling me about,' I replied.

Drake cleared his throat. 'Oh, the Artist's Society of Sanbrisi? Yeah, I know of it. It's part of the main university here. We can take you there. They're enrolling, by the way. Have you any funding?'

I dug out that bag the other Tallis fellow gave me for helping out earlier.

Tallis had a glance. 'What ye got there?'

I spilled the contents out of my hand to show them to Drake and Tallis. The half-assed, crudely hammered coins had spoken their distance.

'I think this should do, Wendie.' Drake returned the coins to the bag and gave it to me. 'But I may consider sponsoring you, if you wish it. Save the coinage for yourself.'

Wow... why was everyone being so generous?

'Thank you,' I blushed intensely.

We walked along the Via Valastra, the main strip of Sanbrisi. I followed slowly, taking in all the white stony marble buildings and statues of naked figures planted everywhere (to make one think something would grow from them). There were sprouting palm trees and fruit trees scattered along the way, and a concentrated mass of people in the centre of the road, hosting *their* market day.

'Doesn't feel like home, does it,' Drake observed.

'No, it's very marbled and ornate. Golden and promising. Most inviting,' I commented. 'Oconnalow is more stone-based in materials.'

'Best material to suit your Irish weather,' Tallis chuckled.

'Guess so,' I sighed, already wondering how my family was getting on.

We hitched upon a wagon ride (which was just as common here, as at home), passing the school on its way to its final stop.

CHAPTER IV

Within the glorious township of Sanbrisi, lived an invading family from Germany called the Gurlskys, whose origins were dubious and quite fraudulent at the best of times.

They started out in the German hamlet of Gasstein, just along the water mark of Melle Broochs (pronounced *brooks*), from different respective families. One of them was called the Berndts, consisting of a mother, father and two children. Slow, peaceful agricultural living in most areas was the order of the day and the Berndts lived an orderly life...

... until their daughter Helena came of age.

She was a boisterous hell-raiser, with an attitude to challenge the pyramids with. Helena was more rowdy when it came to the opposite sex, yet as most of her friends had 'done-it', she hadn't. From peer pressure, she became worse in her jealousy over other people having fun, when she had none. She desperately wanted to play the field, and eventually (on an ice skating rink), she met Albyn Schneide, who belonged to the other respective family. *He wasn't much, but he'll do*, she thought.

The Berndts were horrified at not being consulted about this matching and felt rather uneasy about it. Though the Schneides were prominent businessmen in the neighbouring village of Hansbourg, they got that way through questionable wheelie-dealings. So reservations and rumours began to spread about them...

... and Helena did not like that...

... so she grabbed her lover, Albyn, and decided to run...

... and run, they did.

They ran to the far reaches of their native Germany, past the Melle Broochs, past other towns and villages, where they've been skiving away their lives. The Berndts and the Schneides didn't care where their children were at this point...

... for they knew their kids were old enough and thought it best to fend for themselves.

The starry-eyed, star-crossed couple wanted to get married, and since they were together for some time, it became a strong consideration. In the duration of flight from family, friends and everything else they *knew*, they suddenly ran out of funds...

(*... oh dear, what a shame...*)

... so they marked their next target, the town of Hamilburg...

... and attempted an illegal stint at the local bank...

... posing as a couple twice their age...

... (*though they hardly looked it!*).

Upon seeing Helena and Albyn somehow made up to look old, the make-up spuriously covering their youth, the teller felt a suspicious ring to the situation. He called his supervisor to make enquiries, when at that moment, Helena got violent and punched the poor fellow out, along with a few members of staff and public. She grabbed any and all the loose monies thrown about in the melee, grabbed Albyn (again), and made a further run for it.

They ran and ran for days, and the yearning for marriage crept up within the search of their lives. Being initially of Catholic origin, the couple had approached churches they thought they could get married in...

... but when they were questioned about their residency within the municipality, the answer was quite simple...

... **RUN!**

There was no reply, accompanied by footsteps of heavy meaning and voluminous breathing. You would think these two were unfit at the best of times, with their sloth-like attitudes in life, mooching off the kindness of others, and hustling their way through all areas they passed. Yet, in their far-cried journey, they did come across a building somewhere (*who knew where?*), that adhered to a different and a much older religion...

... *the Old Styler way.*

Helena dismissed any barrier which would prevent her sadistic, controlling nature to be tamed, and barged in upon the unsuspecting arena, with Albyn in tow. He did not enjoy entertaining himself being dragged about by a young independent woman of questionable means...

... *she was alright as a friend, but!*

And thus, with a change of venue of faith, something else needed to be changed. Arrangements were made for a hasty marriage of convenience, and on a dark December day in 1342, they shared histories together...

... within the Old Styler confines...

... presenting themselves under the name of Gurlsky.

In doing so, they fraudulently assumed the mantle as Old Stylers, *without any formal indoctrination,* and just paid the marriage fee, *splitting away from their former identities, religious and otherwise.*

The new name sounded right, they felt, and the tone of this name growled into their satisfaction, much to the disenchantment and tribulation of others.

When it was realised that they could no longer live within German borders, they travelled into Poland, as a fresh new Old Styler couple, and mooched and conned their way into unsuspecting Polish hearts and minds. They always ensured a visit to the local temples to validate their phoney status. Throughout their journey outbound, they caused terror on the scene.

And then they reached Northern Italy...

... entering the once sacred land of the Romans...

... barging past more towns and villages at an enormous rate.

Then, the invading family decided to settle in the fair town of Sanbrisi...

... and took it over...

... through business and community.

Many a day didn't pass without some horrid infiltration on their part. The townsfolk begrudged them and what they represented. Their followers of Old Stylers also settled in Sanbrisi. They kept to themselves, mostly, real quiet-like, and stayed within their own borders of occupation.

A disused building that was planned for other means, was bought intentionally by *that* community, who used it as a place of worship. Homes were made around it, from those forcibly migrating away...

... as it was a better option to live *elsewhere*.

For those who remained, life continued reasonably untouched, unless they tangled with the Gurlskys and their respective community. Word about the family spread, and soon, they started to refer to Helena as the 'Helennic Medusa'. She was tough nuts at the best of times, and difficult to crack at worst. The family had left matters alone in Sanbrisi, which didn't concern them. If anything did concern them or their self-made community, things heated up faster than a re-enactment party between Pompeii and Mt Vesuvius.

The university in the district taught many a fine fellow, and some women were admitted, if they showed promise, or money. A grandson of Sans-Brys (for whom the town was named) continued the family tradition of posing naturally for the art students. One of the Gurlsky's daughters called Susan had enrolled there, showing a gravitational flair toward the arts. Her taste in painting and style blossomed well, under the tutelage of Sans-Brys (the grandson), but her taste in men was a horse of a different colour. She was sick with the fits, brought on by a childhood accident, so her mind wasn't all clear. The medicines and potions she was prescribed for her condition must have affected it...

... and during her time there, she met up with Joseph Silardicus, a good Italian Catholic boy from a malingering mountain afar...

... and the Gurlskys did not like *that*.

Several wranglings later, Susan and Joseph ran off and married anyway, despite the shortcomings. A young one was born from this union, one *Ambrossia Silardicus*, nicknamed Rose.

Unfortunately for the hare-brained couple, the Helennic Medusa found it intolerable that a child was born from this ill-fated union...

... the sudden mismatch.

After a year and some odd months later, it was deemed that Susan was unfit to carry on with Rose, considering the fits she suffered. The Helennic Medusa thus took the child away from her and Joseph, to raise as her own...

... to intentionally bind and gag her within the Old Styler ways.

Yet, Joseph had the last laugh on the bitch, as he took Rose to a church on the other side of the river, and had her baptised Catholic, just as he was...

... then poor little Rose was thrown to the wolves of the Old Styler religion.

Joseph knew he wasn't wanted; the Medusa made it so. She knew she wasn't wanted either, but she didn't care, pushing her weight around like a bull prize fighter. She felt she had to do this, to save face in the community she helped found. It was also to exert control over an innocent soul, and to continue their fraudulent lives as Old Stylers.

Joseph then left Susan in haste, at Helena's behest, and entered into permanent exile. He had no visitation rights to Rose, nor did he ever meet his daughter later in life...

... and the evil that was the Helennic Medusa had renamed the child Rachel, in keeping to their newly-adopted tradition.

He was not pleased with that at all, and fell ill upon the matter.
Later, he consulted with a glass tankard in a local tavern,
Gathering his time and nights away,
With no knights around to save the day.
Oh, did he feel sick that day!
The infirmity of being chased away
By the Helennic Medusa,
With nothing more to say.

The daughter Rachel (*still Rose, but…*), though, had *so much* to say. With an interest in arts herself, she made enquiries to get herself enrolled in the school like her mother did, but in writing courses. Helena and Albyn weren't above a good education for *their* Rachel, and oddly enough, they agreed to it when she came of age.

In the meantime, she was schooled among the Old Stylers, who found her wanting, and too different to them...

... it must be that Italian blood she carried, infused with the German...

... to make one hell of a person out of her.

Rachel felt she didn't fit-in, growing up and she was correct. Kids noted her hesitant, unwilling, and dismissive nature, and teased her about it. It was so obvious that she showed a social incompetence. Her now-adopted family berated her, applying constant pressure to adhere to their Old Styler ways. Everyone else around her had dutifully done so, why didn't she? Yet, Rachel knew she was an oddity among the layman and the scholars...

... but she did not know why.

Rachel found the experience distasteful, torrid, exasperating, and it did not draw her any closer to God than her mother's paintbrush! She felt something was wrong in the mix. The feeling of walking on eggshells around these people (*or were they?*), proved appalling for her, and the heightened sensitivity regarding her true origins was foremost in her upper mind. The fact the young girl's name was completely changed, sent loud bells ringing throughout the district of her understanding.

Why did she feel so punishèd?
When life around her was beyond the shed!

CHAPTER V

The paths lay strewn with late summertime floral beneath us. In the fair wind, I could feel an autumnal chill to come, which I found regularly, living in Oconnalow. The wagon I rode in stopped in front of a building that would become my accommodation.

Drake took out a coin to give it to the driver. The wagon continued its journey forward, and I was led toward another one, inside, up a small flight of stairs. It was a dormitory, full of men in their late twenties (with a few possibly older), aspiring to be artists. The walls displayed the inevitable graffiti of its former and current occupants. This was accepted, since they *were* art students. Bunks lined along the walls of each room, with under bed storage hidden underneath. There wasn't much to go on, as these fellows looked like vagrant layabouts and hobos from the streets, compared to being astute pupils...

... but then again, who was I to judge...

... sometimes a person of such lowly status could become the next genius, if he wasn't one already.

There were about six other guys in the room besides me. Drake introduced us to get further acquainted.

'You'll be in good hands here,' Drake said.

'Thank you for your help and company,' I replied back.

He left me with this new group, for some run along the shoreline no doubt. One of the six approached me.

'So, you're number eight in our little band. I believe you'll fit in well here,' he said.

Embarrassingly, I'd forgotten his name for the moment. To my relief, he reminded me.

'I'm Tarque, the rest are Woodes-Hastings, Tudmond, Wilset, Nay-Smith and Cateliffe. My other friend, Buckingham, is in the next room visiting someone. He won't be a moment.'

I stuck my hand out. 'I'm Wendie.'

Everyone took turns to shake hands, when Wilset asked me, 'Why Wendie? Don't you have a more fuller name?'

'Oh yes,' I replied, 'It's Timoseph Wendel Daye.'

Woodes-Hastings focused on me in recognition. 'Daye, you said?'

'Yes.'

I felt a bit uneasy, but he let me off the hook.

'You give us good business,' he smiled.

Tudmond wondered, 'What's 'e getting at?'

I then remembered the Woodes-Hastings family of Totteringstate, of which one of these fellows was from.

'We've ordered pigs from you, boasted to be the best,' I confirmed.

'My cousin William raves about the orders he gets from you people,' Woodes-Hastings smiled.

I returned the smile. 'We've produced our own, you know.'

Woodes-Hastings came closer to me. 'Get enough of those porkers, you can have your own pig farm, but do not forget, we're the best in the county. Don't sell us out.'

I dismissed the obvious show of pride, when Tarque said, 'Wendie, you'll be sleeping in this bunk with me.'

I had no preferences, but just in case. 'Top or bottom?'

'I've been at the bottom for some time, but if you want it...'

'No sense putting you out. I'll go atop.'

With that, I climbed atop the bed and felt on top of the world.

Tarque noticed my settling down, when he announced to everyone. 'Now, fellas. We're on a challenge. The Sanstratten Chapel needs decorating. It's new on the block, fresh built and our people offered to lend a hand. We will be trained at the college next door. Our skills should reflect the cultural atmosphere of Sanbrisi and of Italy in general. Any questions?'

Woodes-Hastings sniggered within the group. 'So no psychedelic knitting?'

'No,' Tarque answered. 'No knots, no knits, no fairy lights, none of our British craziness. It has to reflect Italy.'

'But what's the point of being an exchange student if we do not contribute elements of our own culture,' Tudmond cried, his Welsh pride firmly in control, but dying to exit its box.

'I'd be happy to help, but need more practise,' I piped up.

'Alright,' Tarque sighed. 'Between our class and the Sans-Brys sculpture class, we'll have all the help we can get.'

'I guess I'm handy with a brush,' came a loud thought from Wilset.

'Good, stick it in your toolkit and be ready,' Woodes-Hastings joked, semi-seriously.

I panicked, feeling unprepared. 'But I don't have a toolkit.'

'It's just a figure of speech,' Tarque explained. 'We'll fix you up with what you'll need. You must provide the rest.'

I gave him a look.

'Your head, your skill. Something only you can personally contribute.'

I exhaled. 'So no Celtic knottery then?'

'Not even knittery,' Tarque said, 'But I will look into it, if it means so much to you.'

'I am but a Celt, you know,' I grinned.

'Look, we're all intermixed ourselves, from all over Britain, and even Ireland,' Tarque explained.

At least I knew I was with the right people.

Buckingham joined us, entering the room. He looked as if he were a tutor, or teacher, but as it turned out, he was just an older kid like the rest, with a well-meaning, patriarchal face.

'Ah, I believe we have a new student among us, willing and eager to learn and help out,' he beamed.

Tarque took me before him. 'This is Wendie. He's from Oconnalow.'

Buckingham's brow ruffled. 'Wendie, eh? Sounds a bit odd.'

'My full name is Timoseph Wendel Daye.'

'A Daye from Oconnalow, wow,' Buckingham chuckled. 'Woodes-Hastings here has a cousin who runs the pig farm at Totteringstate. We're all farm boys here, ain't we?'

Wilset was unfettered by Buckingham's mock-formality. 'I'm not. I am an aspiring artist. I do not wish to be stuck in the mud like my cousin back in Totteringstate. I want to be more cultured than that.'

'Then take a course in science,' Tudmond howled. 'They're looking for things inside small peeping holes to find odd bits in little dishes.'

'You're a right dish yourself,' Wilset hissed back.

'Gentlemen, gentlemen,' Tarque quelled the near-riotous mood.

What snobs! What have I gotten myself into?

'Oh, never mind him,' Buckingham dismissed. 'We're working together. There's always time-off for a little steam.'

'With a little steam, we could create transport around the countryside,' Woodes-Hastings hastily, and loudly, thought.

I wondered, 'But why import British fellows to paint a chapel?'

Buckingham had a ready answer to that...

... in the form of a question. 'Well, why are you here?'

'Well, I was looking for a harbour side job in Queens-Cobhayr, when I wound up on a boat, which led me here.

'You Irish are always looking for opportunity,' Tudmond sneered.

'No different from you,' I quipped back at him, 'Yet, it must be a privilege to work and contribute to a country like this.'

Wilset's snobbery became more notable. 'As a cradle of civilisation, it is a goodly privilege. That's why we are here. To better ourselves, as compared to our pig farming, labouring cousins.'

'Speaking of pigs, I'm hungry,' Woodes-Hastings suggested, getting down from his bunk 'What do you think? Anyone with me?'

Tarque looked at me, concerned. 'Got any money on you?'

I shuffled through my coins, to see there were quite a few of them still left.

'They're worth little amounts. I doubt they'll tender well.'

He examined the coinage carefully, then returned the lot to me.

'Money is money, and this is a port town. The people here expect to be paid with foreign dosh. It'll do,' Tarque assured me.

Then, in the early evening, we went out to a tavern called *Nido dal Petto Rosso*, translated as *The Red-Breasted Nest*.

CHAPTER VI

After a smashing night out, I awoke, feeling on top of the world in my topside bunk.   It was strange, though, not being at home back in Oconnalow, and I'd wondered on how my family was doing. I thought to send a letter to them, or at least a quick message stating that I was fine, living in sunny Sanbrisi, Italy. Maybe the Hopping Drake could help there...

... but now I needed to focus my attention on my task with Tarque's group in painting Sanstratten Chapel.

I got down from the bunk, and walked around. Everyone in the room slept away still, and I could see it was very early, as the dawn arose. I didn't have much on me, but for the clothes on my back, and perhaps a little less money in the world...

... for a night out could do that.

I had no care about that, as I was told the work I'd do for the Artist Society would pay for itself in board, room and minimal upkeep...

... not that I needed much anyway.

I walked unto the balcony, which looked over a small courtyard. Other tenants of the building bustled about in their early morning chores, probably to get them darn over with, before the heat of the sun hit later on. The sun itself began to peek over the horizon and a cool breeze flowed through my linen tunic. Palm trees lined the street around the building, surrounded by other buildings which spread out toward the harbour's edge. I enjoyed the air of Sanbrisi, and I found it to be an enriching township. I was pleased to marvel at it, and contribute to its ongoing beauty.

I could see the Chapel's stout steeple on the next street over. It was a plain square building, built by a Germanic Dutchman called Sanstratten, and nothing like the other churches that littered the town in faith, nor of the Cathedrals of the larger cities. It had the look of want to it, and that was what we were used for... to turn the place into something fantastic for the township to be proud of.

When I volunteered to participate in the project, I was required to attend various classes to train for it, over the next month. I took mostly brushwork tutoring, with a little sculpting, led on by the grandson of the original Sans-Brys, who came over from England about a century ago to teach 'life study'. It was *that* Sans-Brys himself who encouraged foreign students to vary Sanbrisi with a touch of their far-off cultures...

... as he thought that the same look could get too familiar in a surrounding district...

... so, it turns out that my Celtic knottery designs could come in handy for a change!

Along with intensive art classes, the life classes Sans-Brys taught were most extraordinary. He taught with his mind and body, and boy, was he sharp in both. He hadn't batted an eyelid regarding his altogether in front of us, as there were no women present...

... and it was said that *he* was the best.

He just taught, showing muscle definition, and other traits of physical perspective. It was nearly like a science class, because he was so specific about everything. He liked to be known as a 'physical scientist', demonstrating the 'science of the physique'.

His inspiration for *his* art were the ladies of the ancient world, including goddesses of Rome and Greece. He fancied Aphrodite, but his real hook was Venus DeMilo.

During the class, he would at times prattle on about history, too; thus, it became a not-so-boring mix of art, science and history, rolled into one. He was good looking too, and if there were students of *that* persuasion, they'd better hold on to their hats...

... because he was *not*, and I figured he was involved with someone anyway…

… as good looking men don't roll out on a disc alone.

Sometimes our work was done with sculpting, but those with rubbish sculpting skills could simply copy his form in sketching, with the discards making their way onto the walls of many a lady. Overall, Sans-Brys was full-on entertainment, with a huge dose of skill-work needed for our project. He wanted to get Sanstratten painted up with wild, religious and meaningful frescos, allowing for influence from abroad (continuing his antecedent's wish)...

... so much for what Tarque said!

He understood this when I pulled him up on the subject, which showed unawareness of the intention of the original Sans-Brys.

'Oh sorry, I had not known,' Tarque replied, 'I figured they'd go for Italian designs.'

I was most relieved to hear this, and with the skills I learned at school, I felt I could flourish the Chapel with colour and knotted beauty.

The drawing and painting classes, meanwhile, proved rather messy at best, and I got my tunic dirty many a time. They paled in comparison to the *Sans-Brys Hour*, but they were favoured with equal importance. The tutors were reasonable, but lacked the delicious dignity and passionate yearn-to-learn attitude Sans-Brys embodied.

Thus, I invested in a smock to use for the grimy work and one day, I went to the central well to get the dang thing cleaned, when I noticed a young girl in her early twenties walking past me, not too far older than myself. I gazed at her longingly, as she looked afar, distant, yet wanting... *unknown.* The girl shared something of an awkward nature, which stuck out pretty harshly, like a cold winter in August. Her brown eyes, hidden under light golden brown hair, shone above a petite stature. Her small face indicated much on her mind, and her body was loosely covered by a frumpish Germanic dress.

She had a small pad of parchment, dutifully written on; I could not make out the words, or symbols...

... it wasn't my business anyway, so who knew?

She noticed my curiosity. 'They're my hieroglyphs.'

'Hieroglyphs?'

'Yes. Shorthand scribble dried on a page, or something like that. I do it all the time,' she smiled proudly.

'What's your name, lass?'

'Rachel, but call me Rose, please.'

'Rose it is, then. Call me Wendie.'

'Glad to meet you,' she said, noting my smock. 'I can see you're an art student.'

I showed her the smock and put it on. 'You can tell, eh?'

'It looks like a dress on you,' she giggled.

'Only to cover up my tunic with,' I admitted.

Wow, was she absorbing, but most likely self-absorbed. I furthered our conversation anyway. 'What do you take up?'

'Writing classes,' she replied. 'Free verse. This is an assignment I'm carrying.'

She showed me the frenzied parchment of her writings.

'You always write like that? I trust it'd be difficult to read later.'

'Only if I read it after inception to the page. Then I know what's coming next.'

It was too overwhelming to pile me with, and I had enough to do with Tarque and company. *Yet, I wanted to meet with her again and read those parchèd writings!*

'Can I have the pleasure to dine with you tonight?'

'My folks want me to be in early, if I do go out. They're very scrutinising with people I go out with. And if I do go out, I'll not want to come back, if you get my meaning.'

What was I dealing with here? 'Can't say I'd blame you. You're young, as am I. We all want a good time, but you *can* look after yourself, yes?'

Her features changed. 'I can, but they won't let me.'

'Who? Your folks?'

'Yeah, them. Ummm....,' she began to walk away.

'Don't go. I'm sorry I brought it up. You look like you need some support.'

She sighed. 'I could use some. I was adopted by grandparents and they treat me with disrespect, as a child who knows no better. It's frustrating to go out into the wider world, without turning your back to see who's following beside you. It could be them or another member of their family.'

'I'm beside you,' I grinned.

She held my hand. 'I know. But they could be too.'

I took her hand to kiss it, when suddenly, another hand grabbed me from behind and slapped my face. The person who struck me had a face more frightening than Hitchcock's, a tutor I once studied under during thin farming spells. I immediately froze upon impact, *yet I was still alive*.

Then, a gruff voice spoke in a most wildest Germanic accent. 'Don't you ever dare touch that young lady again, y'hear???!'

The newcomer made off with the girl and took her away from me, quite cruelly. I was convinced I'd made a friend of one type and an enemy of another. I knew I had to be careful, because now, I found I was dealing with something seriously over my head...

... and it sure felt nasty.

It wouldn't be the last I would see of her, and maybe I can ask Tarque or one of his group about this unusual personality. With some luck, of which the Dayes have plentifully, I'll overcome this faltering obstacle.

CHAPTER VII

A week later, despite the mock-Hitchcock personage who walloped me, I saw her again anyway...

Rachel-by-the-Well.

Her stature was demeaned, and I saw some discolouration on her cheeks; her face revealed a discrepancy upon her lips.

I felt slightly guilty that it could have been me that caused these questionable features upon her, yet I asked, 'You alright, lass?'

Rachel (*or Rose as I now called her, as she requested*) did not face me; I could not blame her. she fascinated me, as I realised that she deserved a much better place in life than... than...

... oh my Lord, where was she from, and from whom was she?

Rose continued to keep her back to me, as she drew water from the well in silence. Unhappiness clouded her otherwise bright demeanour. Silence could not match the slow dirge that blasted between us. I tried to converse with her anyway; the one stab of the arrow on its target, leaving no shame upon me.

Yet, it was a torment I could not bear, but... *I am a Daye*, I said to myself, *and I do not care who throws me astray. I can pick myself up and fight this... do it, do it, DO IT!!! They cannot harm ye, they cannot grieve upon ye, ah Christ and ye saints, fuck the lot of them!*

Thus forth, I headed into my own destruction...

… and entered the forbidden realm. 'I take it you'd gotten into trouble for seeing me.'

My words fell into some stifled air I could not put my finger on. Frustratingly, she remained quiet... *too quiet.* Then, she looked up to me, and her eyes started to sparkle with hope...

... when she interrogated me with unbridled passion. 'Do you live around here?'

'Yes. A few doors away,' I replied calmly. 'Is there something I should know, or that you wish to see?'

'Ummm,' Rose looked around in a manic frenzy, biting her lip. 'I want to go with you.'

Taken aback, I was stunned to hear such a plea, as we only just met...

... *again!*

She carried on the rampage, continuing to scan the area with a hardened gaze. 'I'll tell you in a safer place.'

I would have loved to assist her in her findings, but I did not know what, or who, to look for. I took her toward the dorm building, knowing I was due to meet at the Chapel for its decoration...

... making my impact with Celtic-knotted psychedelicness on the walls.

'Here,' she led me to an alleyway. A black and white cat with a collar of three bells mewed and hissed, before belting away from its matchbox'd cave.

I turned to face her, demanding, 'Now, what's up with you? What's going on?'

She sighed heavily, exhaling a final breath before sharing more of her story with me. 'My family is on the look-out for me. I said earlier that was adopted by grandparents. They run the syndicate that controls Sanbrisi, and call the shots, much to the municipality's dismay. They have money and bought their way into power, out-doing the local figures. I don't have much; my real family is gone. They ran from my grandmother and got married. My natural father was named Joseph Silardicus, but left, due to the grandmother's attitude and will-power over him. My mother had been ill and recently died. I knew her, but not on a mother-daughter basis. We were like friends. I know, this does not make sense to you. Please bear with it. The grandmother, I fear is controlling my life, to be like the rest of *her* family. I firmly disagree with them and all they believe in and represent. It's a long, tangly yarn... gosh...'

She trailed off, as the wild gestations of her life slowed down to a pulse then, and I was beginning to feel for her. *Her litany of sorrows would make the pages of our prayer books, if they so dared.* My conscience stood harried by the unrelenting pages of *her* experiences and I had to dust the crap off me, before I, too, became entombed by the pain.

Rose spoke more. 'I am young, and I see you are too, maybe older, but we could still be friends, or more, if you get my meaning.'

A quizzical look crossed my countenance. I could have been cruel and told her I had a lover, or a wife, or a steady girlfriend, and that I was unavailable to play rescue-man...

... and not get involved...

... but... I was unattached on all fronts, and certainly sympathetic. I chose to listen further, even help her to some degree. After all, it was someone from Rose's family who slapped *me* on the face previously...

… so, now it was to become personal, and I shall make it so.

'I think we could, but from what you're telling me, you just want to get away from them, really. Is that it?'

'Most certainly, yes,' she uttered. 'With your help. I am sorry my grandmother slapped you. It was out of order for her to do this to you. I hope this does not impair our budding friendship.'

I touched my already bruised-in-the-mind cheek. 'Yea, I am just as sorry, and no, we shall not be unravelled. Yet, truly I say to you lass, I did not come to Italy to be a hero to a proverbially distressed damsel.'

An uneasy pause came between us…

… which I relieved in stating, 'Yet, I am willing to be your friend and, due to your family's obvious hatefulness toward me, destroy their over-controlling impulses that plague your life and possibly hurt mine.'

I stuck my hand out to her. She took it, and asked further, 'Will you free me from this monstrous syndicate?'

'Hold on, before we start untangling the web, I need to find out more about them and their hold on this township. I can ask my friends, who had been here longer than me. Would that suffice?'

'Yes, yes,' she begged, 'Just hide me. How far are we now?'

I looked around the alleyway, into the busy street, and pointed at the building with the stout steeple, 'Just over the way there.'

She freaked out, like I never saw before. 'A church??'

'Yes, a church. I'm doing the decorating. That's why I've come here.'

She looked closer to me, with more intensity, realising, 'Oh, you're not Italian.'

'No. I'm Irish. From the District of Oconnalow.'

The thought of an outsider having to do with poor Rose was too much to bear, as it was just as inviting. Discouragement between the real world and the world of an Old Styler was a vast chasm that most people dared not cross...

... yet I did, just by being with her.

More begging ensued. 'Take me to your friends, please. Quickly.'

'Alright. Alright. Don't get your tunic in a twist,' I insisted.

We then walked away from the hidden passage into that busy street. Luckily, it bustled with activity, yet, under its busy coverage, could lay an enemy from the syndicate who could snatch the lass from under my nose...

... and, as I promised to help her, I would never allow that!

I went to a market stall, and bought a ladies scarf for her to use to hide herself within to be less conspicuous. We carried on our walk, until we made it to Sanstratten.

I took her through the doorway and saw my bunkmates, as well as other students, crowd around the inner walls, putting their British marks on an otherwise Italian landscape.

It was coming along well, when Tarque came up to me. 'Daye, you're late. Take a brush and start work before the head comes around to check up.'

I found some odd brushes laying aside, and grabbed one...

... *then Tarque noticed the girl...*

... and pounced a snap on me. 'And who is this, pray?'

'Oh, this is Rose. I met her outside, by the well. She came to help, too. May we talk aside?'

'Oh very well,' Tarque pouted, and we went to a corner, where I explained her situation to him.

He nearly screamed at me. 'The syndicate??! The Old Styler syndicate???'

I blushed, as she did not reveal what *type* of syndicate her family was, nor had I ever heard the term Tarque used to describe them. 'That's what she told me, but I was unaware of the Old Styler bit.'

'They're a very dangerous bunch. But never mind that. We've got work to do. Maybe she can be of service to us. As long as this place is done up, no one cares who drops by to help, as long as we are the main body doing it. Now, get moving, and get her a brush. Keep her busy and secluded. I'll think of something. Maybe the Hopping Drake could help us.'

The Hopping Drake ... I'd forgotten about him. He's got the ins and outs of this place. He should know of this *syndicate*.

'Doesn't mean she is,' I argued, in afterthought to Tarque's reference to them being dangerous. 'It looks like she wants out.'

'We're here to paint, not rescue someone from unyielding families,' Tarque furthermore snapped under his brushwork.

I looked toward Rose, who stood there with longing and slight haste. She even glanced the doorway, just in case. I gave her a brush and told her to go to a corner and paint that section. She did up and down strokes in her vicinity. It wasn't much, but it made for a good backdrop for overlapping designs to be done later on.

We kept her on, as she diligently worked and stroked obediently.

'She's good,' Tarque complimented. 'When it dries, Daye, you're to put your stamp on it.'

'With pleasure,' I smiled back, thinking of a different kind of stamp to put on *her*.

I was looking forward to continuing where she left off...

... but where she left off from, was another story entirely.

CHAPTER VIII

Meanwhile, the young girl Rachel (i.e. Rose), after the spell at painting the Chapel wall (though not in full), was returning home to *that* family. It was most common that she would go back to them, after any and all journeys she embarked upon outside. It was very restrictive within the home as it was; going out should have been *a respite from it all*, yet it wasn't. So, why she did it, was unknown to most enquiring minds. *Was she desperate? Was she flying with someone? Or did she just want to keep the peace?*

And the answer was...

... all of the above.

She walked through a palatial building on the way, made of glamour and marble. It looked homely, but it wasn't home. The deceptive comfort it depicted was alluring to her, especially as the family were collectors of some sort. Many an hour in the lower levels of the property gave way to further fascination of their lives prior to her birth. It looked a goldmine in there, but it was not worth anything to anyone but themselves. It wasn't fantastically decorated by the Italian artists of the day, either...

... because they moved on to better projects.

The family she returned to were quite degrading to her, and when she spoke to them, they heeded her very little. Chastisements were met with the comment, *'It is just constructive criticism.'* It was Rachel herself who had to engage with them first, in order to get anywhere with them. When there were no telling-offs to be had, they ignored her altogether, unless she was in the altogether with a man...

... this would raise concerns...

... and a steady hand near her face.

The family (most notably the grandparents) were well entrenched within *their* community of followers. They wanted their business dealings to succeed, in order to legitimise their stand there and to save face (assuming there was one to save). The surrounding communities found it difficult to get used to, especially when this family burned with religious fire that consumed all their days. Rachel herself was burned *by* this said fire, and saw that they were too ingrained in the cause of their society to reject it...

... but she did.

Most outside folk hated this family, especially the grandmother Helena, called by locals the 'Helennic Medusa'. The analogy was correct, in that she targeted and caught the fear in all, and Rachel was no exception. Any entanglements with the grandmother on the part of a friend of Rachel, would be met with resistance, and the naturally steady hand-over-the-face, (though in some cases, used as a final resort; to others, well, God help them!). This would constitute an attack upon a stranger; an assault. *But what did it matter to them?* Why should they care about a stranger who *liked* Rachel? They had a low opinion of strangers in the first place, and saw to it that Rachel would never engage with them. If she did, there would be a questioning equalling that between a constable and his prey. It seemed that this was all a front, *but to what end, and to what, to begin with?*

Was the Medusa sane? Could she lip read, or worse still, could she mind read? Mental manipulation was her favourite tactic, and a science which no one had discovered yet. Loving someone, with a catch... conditional love was most likely the case here. *You loved us, or else.*

Some people thought of it as two-faced, which most Old Stylers practiced, along with their oppressive religion. It was a favoured way her followers in her community resorted to...

... but this was no holiday.

The horror the Medusa brought out in people consisted of paranoia walking on eggshells. If the shell broke, there would be a score to settle that no one could win but her. The elder woman enjoyed a good go at control, making others suffer to keep herself intact as self-righteous. On a normal basis, she was not a horrendous figure, but her nature within showed a shell hiding insecurity. Now, you may ask yourself why and what would she be insecure about? The fakery would prove this, yet most people in the community, including their leaders, saw a formidable person at work, with a dedication and skill in her knowledge of their ways. *Did it help the soul inside, though?* It would help if there was one to begin with! The endless, boundless negativity was as gripping as a sordid Greek drama built on the foundation of tragedy. Rachel did not want to get caught up in that...

... and then there were the punishments themselves.

Heavy cartloads of guilt surpassed the smiling face of a once pleasant atmosphere. A wry odd comment would be misconstrued and later regretted on Rachel's part. Sometimes it was true she spoke out-of-turn, or was interrupting a conversation without saying *excuse me*. But this was no excuse to use *to hurt someone deliberately*. This sort of feeling would dig in like a relentless treasure hunter, at it in the crypts of the ancient world. The guilt would then penetrate the surface, taking the harsh, subliminal leap toward brainwashing. This led to Rachel's insecurity in her own existence.

The feeling she was not wanted, the feeling of being unloved without the catches had haunted the young girl with a ferocity like that of a storm upon a desert island. Horror seeped into the conscious being, making someone look around frantically in a market square, or any ol' square, when the will permitted. And, you would think that in a busy place, no one could see your face among the hundreds of the millers-about...

... but think again.

If the brain stood still in its firmed stance, the next step proved to be the most gruesome-most kind of trepidation...

... the candle wax.

Though this treatment wasn't the only tendency toward the violent end, it was a strong one, with emphasis, by many means.

Before Rachel was born, one of the Medusa's children who, when younger, fell foul of misdeed and got himself into a fix-on-the-lips. The other children watched, as he was slowly subject to submission-by-candle wax...

... and later in life, he became lame-in-the-brain, living the life of a mental exile...

... and then this happened to Rachel herself.

It was mostly a minor incident (a silly thing that happened during the school day when she was very young), and a most unnecessary reaction to it. A known boisterous child, thrust into the whims of the Medusa due to circumstance, she was subject to a most ghastly experience...

... but she resisted the mental breakdown and recovered fully...

... only to set her sights upon the better things in life, belonging to the *outside* world.

So, Rachel wanted a piece of the action; *no holds barred for her.* When she met the kind young man that was me, she grew fascinated with my company. The well in the square made a good meeting place, and she enjoyed the time she spent with me, however little that may be. She was willing to go, again and again, just to defy that horrible syndicate, where *that* family was in control.

The Medusa spoke hard words to her, when spies informed the grandmother of Rachel going into a church. This was the most forbidden action to an Old Styler. It was regarded as a blasphemy to their own kind and belief structure. It was a place beyond *their* control, and it was control they wanted to use upon Rachel. Yet, the Old Stylers served no other purpose, but to disrupt the flow of goodly faith...

... which at this point was emerging in Rachel.

The syndicate and the Medusa had regarded all outsiders as NOSSers (Non Old Stylers; the final 'S' didn't stand for anything, but made pronunciation easier). They hated them and discouraged any to co-mingle with them. It was a frenzied life for Rachel, and one she could not understand. The attraction of the NOSSer charms proved unrelenting for her. Curiosity may kill a cat, but it never faltered for Rachel. Her endless daydreaming, away from Old Styler whims, had left her wanting more and becoming more isolated within *that* family and community. She was growing up, half-decently (to some level), the other half being part of the degenerate syndicate that was blighting the landscape of Sanbrisi...

... but how could you defeat these rotters?

It was obvious that Rachel did not see eye-to-eye (or head-to-head, for that matter) with the rest of *that* family. Her Italian father's blood, flowing inside her, saw to that.

It was also the blood that screamed the loudest for her, making her see another destiny. She never gave in to such terminal nonsense, and let the bull-shitters of impractical belief roll away to the other side of her mind, hoping their nonsense would fall out of her ear. She was determined to improve herself, by hook or by crook. She suddenly realised by her late teens that all *that* family was doing, was to justify its existence in the Old Styler's world...

... as *small* as it was.

Yet, it was there, lurking within failed societies of yore, ready to be plucked into submission, causing mishap and trouble for many. Again, they were too ingrained in the cause of their society to reject these actions. Most people grew tired of the fuss and the hassle and allowed livelihoods to be overrun by *that* family syndicate. Using legality, the syndicate punished those who were against them, usually putting them to the sword, or using more psychological means, as aforementioned. The psychological path was more fun for them, as manipulation was their greatest asset. No one would (or could) mess with the syndicate. Those in even higher power felt it was the town's problem, not a nationwide crisis...

... so it was let be...

... until the mix of Italian and German came along to (hopefully) free the town of this riotous insult...

... not knowing this lovely mix of a girl would be going undercover for the glory of the Lord.

But in the current instance, the Medusa held Rachel firmly in her grip, tighter than ever, pulling the strings, even the more intimate ones...

... when Rachel realised that something-was-up with them, suspecting *a foul misdeed done to her.*

It was that young Irish lad (that was me), who would help in this cause of her plea. Rachel would seek me out, perhaps for her own comfort and happiness, beyond the harried call. I provided a hopeful comfort to her, and she witnessed her grandmother's strike against me. She knew I would be the one to help out. She wanted to run away with *me*, as her mother did with Joseph Silardicus. She was craving to leave *that* family, as she now desired a committed mental distance away from them. Once her plan went through, she would get her original birth name (which she knew was *Ambrossia Silardicus*) restored to full use, and to prove that she was not an Old Styler in the first instance...

... for just because her mother was, did *not* make her one...

... *as most people had the right to choose...*

... *as did she.*

Her semi-perfect eyesight had a twenty-something perspective on it. She believed she was right, because their odd behaviour was not patterned like anyone else's. To slow-boil in negativity, and to be made like you were in trouble ALL of the time as an indefinitely bad person, was too much to take on as a child. Yet, to gain proof of the nonsense would be difficult, without getting further ensnared by the Medusa and the syndicate's fraudulent way of living.

She must tell someone... she wanted to tell me how important it was for her to report these misdoings, and to throw off the evils of the OSS (Old Styler Syndicate). She decided to leave that dowdy marble building, and ran for the nearest exit. Luckily no one was around; she felt sort-of safe...

... the door was there, and she opened it gently...

... found the way OUT, to jet outside in the greatest haste.

Now, where was she to find me? It was logical that I was at the Chapel, doing the decorating. She looked around the streets, retracing the steps she took previously. Leading herself in memory, she recalled the pointing at that stout steeple, and she headed for it, gasping and grasping for the unchanging freedom she was entitled to...

... the steeple's cross marked a beacon which was to determine her fate for the rest of her life...

... with the ability to quash the psychological deformation trying to enclose the boundaries of her soul.

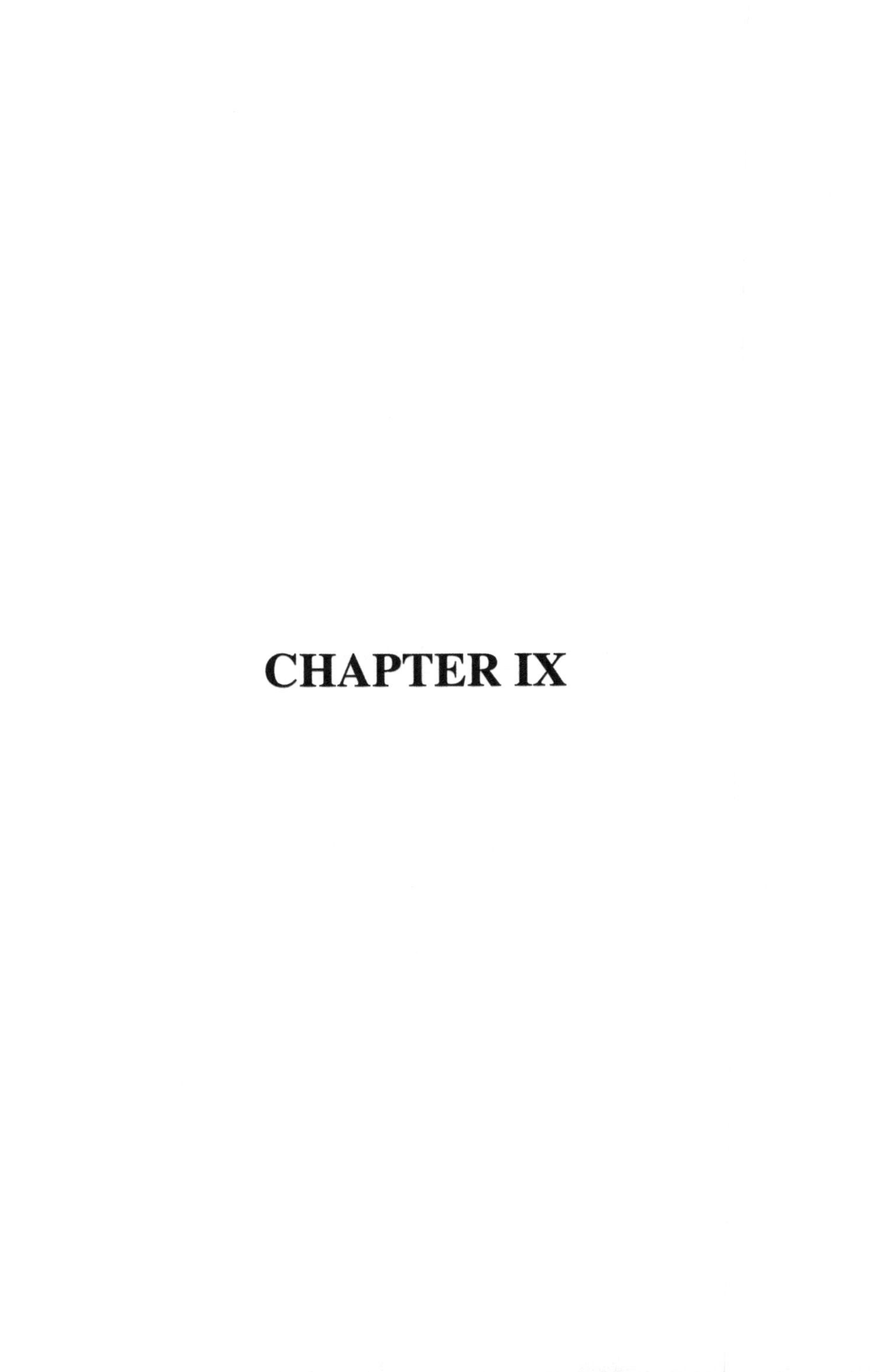

CHAPTER IX

I later sought out the Hopping Drake at the tavern, the *Red-Breasted Nest*, along with my friends from the dorm room. There was much to discuss, with this business with Rose. As time went on, I felt further remorse for her and her plight. How on God's greenest earth could *anybody* be treated in such an objectionable manner? I was also tinged by that misguided slap-on-the-face I received from a complete *stranger. Was I so rotten? Did I look a mess?* Was the slap given to me over *something I represented to Rose*, that the older woman took exception to? I needed the explanations to clarify what went on with that girl!

After a few rounds of wine and decent fare (which could never compare to Mother's), I broached the topic of Rose to the Drake.

'So what about her?' he asked, 'You in love with her?'

'Well,' I began, hesitating. 'I am beginning to see her point.'

'And what point is that, pray,' Drake continued.

I took in a breath. 'The grandmother slapped me. I did nothing wrong, to my knowledge. I was having a peaceful, calm moment with her, then someone viciously took me aside and told me in a few words to back off. The slap was to emphasise *their* point, possibly in representation.'

'Now, Daye, you are getting philosophical. It is either here or there. There is no in-betweens,' Tarque insisted.

'There are always in-betweens, Tarque,' Drake said, 'Wendie is correct. A slap could just be... a slap. Or it could be much more. You take it in yourself. '

'You take it in, mate,' Tarque snapped, being a few years older than us in arrogance. He turned away, showing a look of concern. 'I observed that she seemed wanting. I reckon her family had put her up to submissiveness. The grandparents must be at the bottom of it.'

'It will take more than one voyage to solve it,' Drake suggested sourly, 'Infiltration might be the best solution, with a chance of getting the girl out of there. The syndicate had been controlling businesses around Sanbrisi for many years, since the arrival of these Old Styler Germanic invaders. *They claim to be of the Old Styler way, but they are not.* They are just fraudsters out to make a fast one and pull another one on their own, i.e. this Rose girl you keep on about. Her real name is *Ambrossia Silardicus*; I guess the Rose bit comes from that. When her father was chased off by the mother's family (i.e., the grandmother), and the mother herself had taken ill and died, Rose was at *their* mercy upon adoption. *They even forced her to undergo a name change to theirs.* It is obvious she detests their treatment of her, though they do take decent care of her in the physical sense. It is her emotional and mental well being I am wondering about, IF that is still intact.'

After a quick sip, Drake continued. 'Their hold on the girl is stifling. I've seen them in public with her, and other members of the family spy on her when she's out on her own. It's dreadful. They've bought the municipality off and no one says a word about the injustices they've been getting away with for years, especially in regards to Rose.'

Woodes-Hastings threw his opinion to the wall. 'And he loves the wench, don't you, Wendie? He'll play the hero.'

I sat in silence, nearly in tears, quietly listening to what Drake had revealed to us. I wanted to put my head down and cry, but with all the manliness about, I knew that would lead to poor action...

... so I held my breath in, swallowed whatever tears and fears I had inside, and kept on drinking.

Woodes-Hastings then saw the sadness I expressed and put his arm around me, as I suddenly exploded with dire melancholia. 'We'll get her out some time soon. But we must plan for it.'

'Plan,' Nay-Smith blurted out, 'Plan? We cannot even plan a wedding! How will we go up against this syndicate?'

Drake asked, 'Your people are working on Sanstratten Chapel. Maybe she can join you. It'd take her away from them.'

'Yes,' Tarque answered, 'There's much to be done, and Rose did help us out for a short spell. She's good, when she is able to express herself.'

'But she's no paint brush,' Drake sighed, 'Her mother had that skill.'

'I saw some writing she carried, when I first met her at the well,' I recalled, still fighting my tears.

'We must get her away from *that* family. A flower by another name...'

'... stinks worse than a dung heap,' I interrupted Drake, finishing his sentence, still dripping with repugnance.

'Wendie, that's very true,' he agreed.

'Takes one to know one,' I tried to smile at him. 'I've been on the farm.'

'As we once were,' Wilset intoned, 'That's why we're here. To escape farm life for a better place. It suits our cousins more than us.'

'Hear hear,' Buckingham chimed.

'So you people bettered yourselves through another culture,' Drake enquired.

'It widens the prospects in the world,' Tarque reflected, 'It is hot, the classes are good and with friends like this bunch, it's amazing.'

Everyone clinked tankards in full agreement and comradeship...

... while I moaned about. 'I still want that girl!'

My head hung heavy, as I attempted to carry on enjoying the company I kept...

… but I wanted *her!*

The glass laid empty before me. The bitterness remained on my lips, but it wasn't from the drink itself. Love left a bitter taste in the mind, and all I kept thinking about was Rose. I soon grew desperate for her, and the means by which I would (or could) destroy *that* family and *their* syndicate...

… then I can return to Oconnalow a *man.*

However, I did not think this was what my folks had in mind for me. I knew they wanted me to mature, yet I could hardly think of what they would do, if they found out I was humiliated in public by a complete *stranger.* And I knew they would never, ever experience what I came up against…

… *and it rubbed me the wrong way.*

I sorely missed my lot and quietly asked Drake to send out a quick word to them, using one of the ships heading toward Ireland that I was alright, and I would be back soon. He acknowledged the request, and I nearly fainted in relief.

'Hey, steady on, mate,' Tudmond said.

Buckingham, even older than Tarque, shared a bit of wisdom. 'Cruel foraging in the dark, shines a light on one's own stupidity.'

I looked at the older man. 'What the heck's that supposed to mean?'

'I have no clue myself. So sorry. It's paraphrased from a young poet, a girl, I believe,' Buckingham thought aloud, 'I think it's that Rose of yours. She had a quick spurt in the columns and I read them. She's very good; a mindful poet.'

'Now, you're teasing me,' I taunted, blue eyes staring at the ready.

Buckingham stood firm. 'No, I am not. If you get past her squiggles, you might find she's alright.'

I pressed on. 'You met her?'

'Ummm, not directly,' he said, 'But I'd like to, IF you can get her out of the familial mess she's in. I'd gladly help, but I'm a bit, you know.'

'You're not old,' Cateliffe muttered, 'You're as good as the rest of us.'

Buckingham blushed. 'No, no. Do go on.'

Drake needed to steer the talk to reality. 'Wendie, do you think you can be our infiltrator?'

I stared at him, marked with determination, after all the self browbeating. 'I shall fight for her to the last. I'm a Daye, I'm Irish and I can do it.'

'Suit yourself,' Tarque scoffed, 'If you really want her that badly, she's your prize.'

'Don't come crying to me, if she turns out to be a handful,' Cateliffe warned.

'Or an empty vessel,' Wilset added.

'Oh come now,' I protested hotly, 'She's an interesting girl. Quiet, intelligent, alluring, and I want to distress that grandmother some.'

'She's plain, Germanic and looks rather sheepish,' Nay-Smith mumbled.

'You would be, if you were thumb-pressed! BUT she is the daughter of Silardicus, a descendant of the great Roman general.'

Nay-Smith carried on. 'So she's Italian too, so what?'

The cool, calculated mixing of heritages was something not to be underestimated; I thought much of that about Rose, and I felt it made her to be a well-rounded individual. So, I wanted to give that fellow a hiding for that comment, when Tudmond asked, 'Has she been sold to the Old Styler's ways?'

'Don't think so,' Drake uttered. 'Her demeanour looks as if she's desperate to escape it. You shouldn't judge.'

'I want her to be mine,' I called out. 'And I bet you there *is* more to Rose than what you think. So there!'

I stuck my tongue out, and Drake gave me a look. 'Don't fret lad, we will find out. You'll have her.'

'Possibly more, too, if you think about it,' Tarque advised, grinning.

'Nothing fits, though, and there is something I sense in her. Maybe you can dig further, Drake,' I said.

'I've got the name. I can go check the records, even church records. If her father was Italian, a baptism might have been performed before the grandparents took her away,' Drake suggested.

'Guess that's a start,' Tarque exhaled. 'But we've got a chapel to dress up. Gentlemen.'

Everyone got up and started to disperse. I walked toward the door. I was downcast, and feeling nearly as sheepish as Rose was. The information whirled in my head, it made me sick with feeling, and a firm determination to get this girl for myself, despite the viciousness that was thrown at her.

Tarque caught up with me. 'Where are you going?'

'To find my flower,' I answered, and left the tavern.

I walked away in silence, hoping they'd forgive my action, as the rest of the group went back to Sanstratten.

CHAPTER X

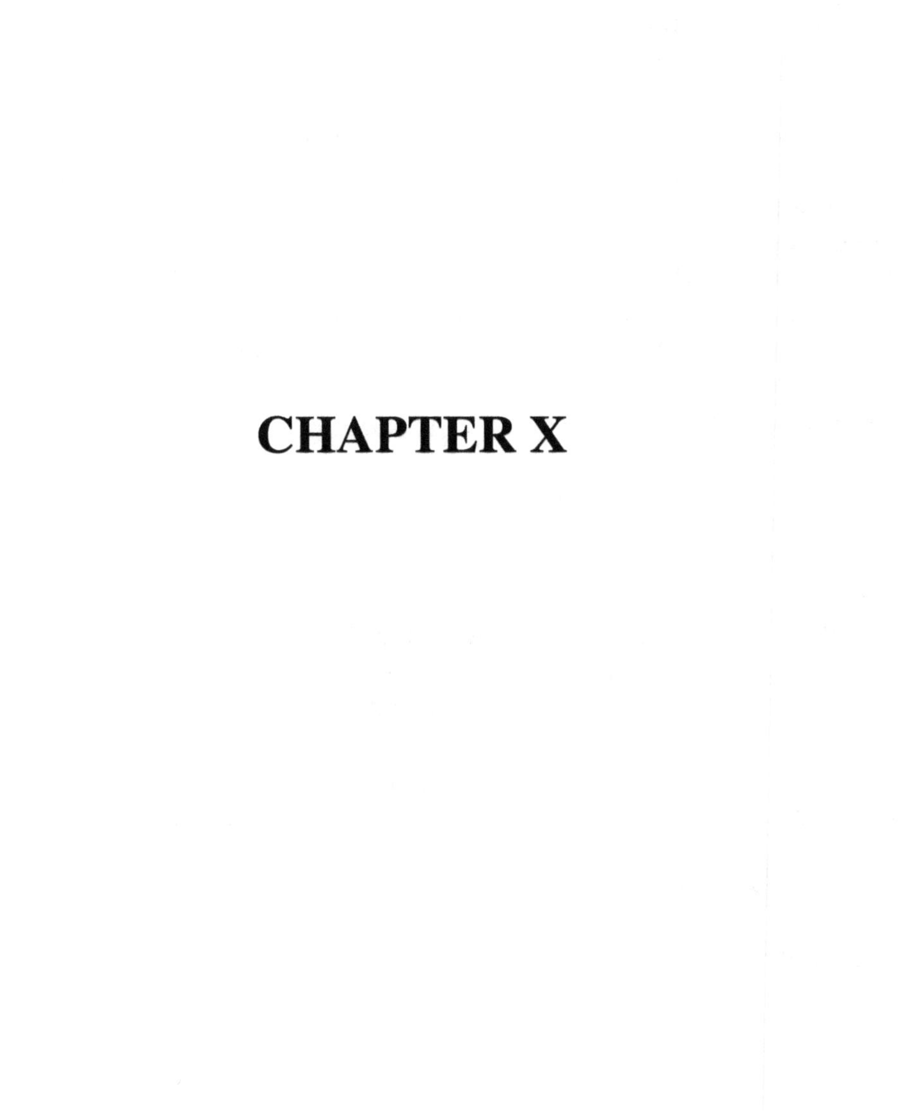

It would be awhile before I found her. And when I did, a few streets henceforth, her family surrounded her like wolves upon a lamb. I flinched when I saw her, so hating the sight, and hid myself under the cowl of my beige light-woollen cloak. Eager to avoid making eye contact, I stayed where I was, while *that* family and the throng outside, entered a makeshift, multipurpose building that served their community. Its imposing, sandy coloured pebbled stonework dominated the end of a street...

... it would also dominate the end of a young lady, if I didn't face up to this.

I followed them in, like the spy that I was, just like the Hopping Drake suggested. I guessed if I wanted to play hero, I had to be in the thick of it! So, I snuck in with the rest of the folk, thankfully unnoticed. There were a few dozen or so people of all ages there, but it featured mostly the older set. They were very chatty; speaking and milling about. I could not make out the language, but it sounded Germanic. They did share the cause of a marked authority in the town...

... but I knew it wouldn't last long...

... if I had something to do with it!

I walked with the rest of the crowd up a flight of stairs to a large room. It appeared to be a sanctuary. Rows of blue cushioned seating laid in the centre of the room, separated in the middle, with stairs leading to some kind of altar. Up there, a pair of doors housed (what I thought was) a secret mini-chamber. God, if I only had some form of communication, I could tell Tarque and the others where I was at present...

... oooh, the frustration of it all!

I hid in the back rows, still unassuming within my cloak...

... and I found that cloaks had a way to disguise the unassuming.

I looked around to find my Rose, spotting her sitting next to...

... you got it, *the grandmother! UGH!!!!!!!*

With nervous fingernails at my chest, I scratched an itch, as I itched to press forward to engage with her...

... no matter what the cost was...

... *but I was not as stupid as that!*

The person next to me gave me a book, which was written in a very calligraphic and curvy manner...

... *much like their tongue, no doubt.*

I was assured this was not Latin, which I was used to in church, but I rode it out into the sunset, trying to *look* the part. I did not care to see what it was, I just followed in their coarseness. Some bits did ring familiar to me, but was expressed in a wholly different manner. The chanting was likened to monastic style, but *of a more hypnotic, droning manner, as if to brainwash its subjects.* As I was unaffected, I took it as part of my education and left it at that. I could not understand it anyway, so it made no additional meaning for me. Thus, how could I fall under its power or allegiance? Rose seemed like she was immune to this, as I was.

When everyone stood up, I hovered about, trying to get to her. I watched her, jittery and wandering still around her seat, fidgeting to escape.

I felt so sorry for her, and it gave me more of a purpose to help guide her away from all this. Misguided as these folks were, I made a firm decision to get her away from these back streets and to be with me for good. I knew she wasn't going to buy all this, not for love or money. *Her family was her family, but they were not forever, if she chose otherwise.*

I made contact with her alone, she nodding in response, before returning to 'paying attention.'

The grandmother glanced my way to see what the fuss was about. She had seen me, yet remained silent. I turned affright for a moment, thinking she would remember the slap-face incident that *she* caused, and recognise me as a friend of Rose's…

… yet she didn't, and returned to *her* unassuming ways of 'follow the sheep'…

… *don't insult the sheep, though.*

I endured this meeting (or service) for some time, and I thought to myself to wish to get the heck out...

... but then I'd lose the Rose...

... and I cannot allow that.

So, I sat there, as uncomfortable as she, stepping into her shoes, as it were (*though my feet were much bigger than hers*). Even bed bugs felt more pleasurable, than being among *this* group of people. Longing to get out, and nearly falling asleep to the ranting rave of foreignness I ever did witness...

... I had realised that it was no wonder the lass wanted out of this shit...

... potentially unnatural as it was for her.

What could I do? I remained steady and followed the leader, so-to-speak, for *I* was no sheep. My mind wandered toward my missed home at Oconnalow, with my parents and sister probably worried sick over me. Growing up was one thing, but to grow up incommunicado was something even I would disapprove of. I was honestly scared that I went in too deep over my head and pushed too hard, in the name of my love. IF there was a speedy way to say 'hello, I'm alright, folks', I'd do it. *Had Drake sent the message? God, I hope so!* It was odd that the grandmother didn't lead this unholy menagerie of oddness. Leading a whole community would be a challenge, even for someone of *that* ilk. Fortunately, they didn't allow womenfolk leadership, as it looked more paternal than anything, but *she'd* most likely have the balls to pull it off...

... as she'd done with one *Ambrossia Silardicus*.

There I sat down, with the rest of *that* brood. I closed my eyes, praying the prayers of my *own* heart. My soul was searching inside, in the only way it knew how, without calling to attention that there was a mere outsider in the midst. No one fretted about me, nor did they invite a scene. Everyone was *wrapped up tight in their own ideologies* (pity), which is something no one should mess with (but concern would be the order of the day, had it been a different circumstance). I was relieved that I wasn't a bother (yet); my thoughts still recurred toward departure...

What held me here? Was it the chanting (similar to our ways, but in another tongue)? *Was it my turn to witness this everlasting boredom and repetition of alien verbiage?*

I guessed it was just me being the infiltrator, the longer I stay, the more information I could pick up. *Would the information be useful to us*, I wondered. Distaste was placed firmly unto my mind, as the droning about continued. I really did step heavily into a pile of strewn, left behind by a multitude of animals. Luckily, *that* sort of strewn would not be everlasting. A good washing up would sort the stain out…

… but the stain on the soul was another entity entirely.

The sympathy toward Rose to go further here, than it would upon the unblemished...

... but this sort of blemish was too much to bear.

Suddenly, the congregation had stood up again for something. I could not see what. *Strewth! I did not care.* I decided to quietly make a break for it. My breath got quieter, as I gently scurried along the wall, away from the people, and found the exit point. Rose shot a look at me, to find me sneaking away. *Oh God, she started to follow...*

... then a family member stopped her to ask where she was going.

The delay cost her time, as she tried to make an excuse to use the outdoor toilet. When they saw through this, they held her back. *They knew she was trying to leave the place.* For a vital second, she would have been set free, and into my arms…

… but no…

… she gave into her defeat and left it alone, remaining at the service.

Oh Rose, couldn't you be brave for a mere…?

I stood at the doorway, still hidden, hoping she'd come out. I nearly wet myself in anticipation, yearning for a glance of my budding warrior princess. *But no... again, but no.* Her fear got the better of her, as the grandmother's hide had shrouded her being, and sight from me.   I wanted to call out, to scream, to yelp away...

... Rose, Rose, ye come with me, baby!

I peeked inside to find her still within the restrained familial conclave. The restraint was too painful to watch and my heart began to crawl with vengeance...

... vengeance against the family, these surroundings, the syndicate...

... and above all...

... *that* grandmother!

I sighed, and left the building, determined to fight it out later, with a bit of luck, and with the many friends I had recently made since my arrival here.

CHAPTER XI

I ran along the silken streets of Sanbrisi, grateful to have left the ordeal I was self-subjected to. I knew it meant nothing to me, and all I could do was draw a blank...

... but there was something else I could put a paintbrush on.

The emotional turmoil was intense and very driven within the syndicate. *That* family which upheld it, drew me a bore. I was not impressed. I reckoned Rose wasn't either. That much of what she was being subject to (through suppressive means), obviously did not register with her either. *Her partiality lay elsewhere.* The whole of what I experienced was hidden behind lyric and rhetoric, and if you were not privy to the scene, you would never understand it...

... which was probably the point of their game...

... something misunderstood, or not taken in well, could be twisted and mistranslated within that calligraphical lettering of another language.

I could now understand what Rose was up against, and why she was being put down all the time...

... in order to satisfy the whims of a *fanatical* grandmother...

... who was trying to hide a *previous identity* that was not based on the Old Styler religion.

I knew I would need help, and lots of it. I had feared though, that Tarque and the others would dismiss all this and tell me to get on with Sanstratten. I felt I was up against something here, too, but it was of a more purposeful insistence. Yet, I carried on my journey toward the dorms, where I figured the others would be taking a break from painting.

I found the building and stepped inside. Woodes-Hastings stood in the doorway of the room, drinking out of a tankard.

He asked, 'Where've you been, Wendie? We've waited and wondered about you. Some of us are still at Sanstratten, you know. I came back to see if you would turn up. You are cementing yourself as being a layabout.'

I shook off some outer detritus that got on my cloak, yet the inner detritus was unfortunately still in my memory. 'Please forgive me. I took Drake's advice and went into the syndicate's realm, looking for the girl. I have something to tell you all.'

'You *had* infiltrated the syndicate? Wow,' he exclaimed. 'I apologise for the comment. It seems that you have been busy.'

'Yes, but I would rather have been busy at Sanstratten with you guys. Can ye get the others here?'

'We'd have to go there. Everyone is working now. I stayed behind, in case you showed up.'

'Thanks,' I blushed firmly. 'Let's go out there. We'll talk on the way.'

'Leave it for the Chapel.'

Woodes-Hastings offered me his drink, which I imbibed most graciously...

... after that experience, whooo!

We went back to Sanstratten, where the students were developing their styles on the walls.

The place looked ornate and most colourful, making even the least intelligent person who prays here, understand Biblical events and stories. The surrounding twirls and curls of colour ornamented the scenes, and sculptures were taking shape in marked corners of the building. It was a whirlwind of fascination, tuned in for religious devotion. Despite the volume of loudness displayed, I foresaw Sanstratten turning into something very beautiful, indeed.

'You stay here,' Woodes-Hastings advised me, 'I'll get the others. They'll be most interested in your findings.'

I waited for them, when I noticed Sans-Brys himself looking over a marble statue. It wasn't based on him, as it was not a nude, but the face showed the formality which Sans-Brys based himself on...

... and I thought it was a fitting tribute to him anyway.

'Hello there,' I greeted him.

Sans-Brys looked at me, over his narrow-lens spectacles. 'Daye, is it?'

'Yes, Wendie Daye.'

'You've been late here in recent times. Is there anything the matter?'

I gulped hard, as the others came 'round...

... being in front of greatness was no mean feat.

'I, I,' I stammered, 'I saw the girl.'

I nearly fainted in thought when Tarque demanded, 'Woodes-Hastings told me you have something to report. You've been in the syndicate's domain, haven't you, looking for that girl? You should have been *here*, working.'

Sans-Brys tried to soothe the moment. 'Steady, Tarque. Let the lad here tell us what happened.'

Innocently, Tudmond asked, 'What's it like?'

I turned to him. 'You sure you want to know?'

His eyes looked a-fright. 'You *have* seen her.'

'I have yes,' I began, 'There was a service there. I attended it covertly, so I went unnoticed. She was sitting with her family, but it was most apparent she was distressed. She even tried to follow me outside, using the old 'outbuilding of convenience's sake' excuse, when her family held her back. She stayed behind, and I had a most suffocating time there.'

Sans-Brys was surprised. 'They can't do *that* to a young girl, preventing her from using a convenience. It is absurd!'

'The family thought she was making a run for it,' I offered.

Tarque pressed, 'And was she?'

I faced him with intent. 'Duh! Wouldn't you?'

He met his defeat with dignity. 'Point taken.'

'Most unfair,' Cateliffe remarked.

I continued, 'They chant like monks but in a foreign tongue I could not make out. The ideology that filled the air was stifling. The duration of the blasted thing felt like purgatory! I couldn't even last three seconds, but for the girl. I wanted to see what turned her tide.'

'And it's a most sinister turn every moment,' Sans-Brys quipped.

'At least I was well hidden under my cloak,' I said, 'Other people were wearing something similar, so I blended in. Everyone was tightly wound in their purpose there, so I caused no disturbance. It was an emotional hell, with no outlet to breathe, used figuratively, of course.'

'I see,' Buckingham interjected. 'Everything is figurative. It depends on your outlook. We've done quite some work here. How's about a spot of lunch?'

'Suits me,' Tarque agreed. 'Sans-Brys, would you care to join us?'

The respected teacher grew red on his very pale cheeks. 'Go on, if you insist. I like to get to know my students on the same parallel.'

'It'd be an honour to have you with us,' Nay-Smith smiled.

'Oh, by all means, though I think you've seen enough of me,' Sans-Brys giggled, blushing.

'We can discuss this further at the *Nest*,' Tarque suggested.

We went out of Sanstratten, to go to our favourite tavern. There, as we ate, we carried on our conversation.

'So you weren't seen, and no one asked anything of you,' Tarque confirmed.

'I think the grandmother saw me, but said nothing. No one approached me,' I answered, 'Not even to throw me out as an outsider. They could not tell the difference.'

'You must meet with her again, and this time, we'll help you,' Buckingham stated. 'She's at that well in the square, right?'

'Occasionally she is,' I said.

'Remember Daye,' Tarque insisted, 'We're letting you do this for your love of this girl of yours. We are not here to rescue her, nor this township. We are here to work on Sanstratten. Got it?'

'I do, and I accept your terms,' I nodded, 'But please, let me have her.'

'Gosh darn, she's yours for the taking,' Buckingham huffed, slightly irritated by my obsession of the girl. 'Be done with it!'

I made my own suggestion. 'We have an opportunity to make a difference here. Once we have Rose, we can take down the syndicate, save the town, and have painted Sanstratten, all at the same time.'

'Tall orders command tall ships,' Tarque got up and paced about. 'But we ain't got any. You're on your own, kid.'

Nay-Smith spoke between bites. 'Eight men from the British and Celtic Isles up against a wild community of no-sorts? That's as unlikely as spilled milk in a tavern.'

I exhaled a deep sigh, feeling left out, feeling more isolated in my quest, feeling just as short-changed as my Rose.

Tarque noticed my complexion and came over to me, putting his arm around me in support. 'Look, it is not like we don't want to help you, or this Rose of yours, but we are up against bad odds.'

Suddenly I had an idea. 'When we complete the task at Sanstratten, doesn't a dignitary come over to dedicate it or something, maybe bless it, as it is a chapel?'

Tarque rubbed his chin. 'I suppose so.'

Sans-Brys looked up. 'I think I can help you there. I had written to the Vatican to bring out a representative. A deputy of some sort to do the Pope's bidding, and all that. I can add this little quandary to my petition. With enough evidence, this deputy might help overthrow the syndicate's hold on this township.'

'And maybe their hold on the girl, too,' I hoped.

'But they've been here for years,' Woodes-Hastings argued. 'One cannot put a stop to them suddenly.'

Sans-Brys added, 'It will not be sudden. Vatican bureaucracy takes time, but the urgency may send him flying our way. Don't worry about it. I'll take care of things at my end.'

'By the way, Rose's real name is *Ambrossia Silardicus*,' I stated.

'Then all the more reason to hope for,' Sans-Brys smiled. 'Are there any records on her, like birth or baptism?'

'Drake's looking into that,' Tarque said.

'I'll get in touch with him,' Sans-Brys offered, 'Meanwhile, Daye, go get your woman!'

After our meal and drinking time, we dispersed back to Sanstratten with agendas on our minds...

... but for me, just a little rosebud of activity will do.

CHAPTER XII

My own life progressed further in the splendid making of Sanstratten. The place was looking exquisite, as it took shape with all the designs us Celts and British combined in our effort. Tarque oversaw the project, like a foreman, but Sans-Brys was the brains behind it all; in charge of the whole ideal...

... as idealistic as he was.

Colours splashed about the walls, telling the old Biblical stories we all heard about as children. My makeshift Celtic patterns were woven into the backgrounds or within the clothing of the characters, to give worshippers and tourists alike, something to think about (perhaps talk about).

The communication Sans-Brys mentioned earlier regarding the Vatican had paid off, and the Pope himself was keen on the Sanstratten Chapel. He planned a visiting envoy, consisting of a representative, Brandoni (along with his underling, DeRino), who could act on the Pope's behalf. Not only would he be dedicating the Sanstratten Chapel, but it was further hoped that he could assist us to rid Sansbrisi of the Old Styler syndicate, which had plagued the region for a few decades.

As I carried out my work, I was thinking of Rose and how she was doing. Word was out that she'd not been seen in recent weeks, except to that odd service I attended, to show face within *that* community. After all, if there was something wrong, it was never mentioned, nor discussed openly. The family dragged her everywhere, just for show, so no questions would arise from anyone else therein.

The grip got tighter upon her, and life became more challenging. She was young, but not as to be so easily led about. Yet, the grandparents had led her about anyway, but only within *their* social circles.

Begrudgingly, she spent much of her social time among those who did not really care for her, in a youth group in *that* community. It was shown thus, as they never invited her to any parties or special personal events. Yet, there was always space for *another*; never her. The grandparents thought it was due to an unfriendly nature she continually exhibited by not smiling. It was not that there was intention on Rose's part to be unsociable. It was just an uncomfortable nature in the environment she grew up in, and the people around her proved unfavourable. She was desperate to have some sort of friend, but to no avail. Misinformation guided the way here, and to Rose's misfortune, many people her age had thought ill of her. *Heaven knew what the adults thought...*

She was grounded otherwise, due to her earlier behaviour of walking into Sanstratten Chapel...

... whereby she was obviously noticed, no doubt getting an earful.

She even stopped attending those writing classes, as the family got too curious about her whereabouts after the lessons, as well as a further interest as to what she was writing. The family also kept tabs of who she was making associations with. Thankfully, her life was secluded enough that there was not much to tell. They mostly left her alone at best, leaving her do what she wanted...

... as long as she was under *their* roof.

It made no matter to me, for I knew her time with them was numbered. I felt she had a chance at life itself, IF she could get away from *that* family. I sorely missed not seeing her by the well anymore, as my desire to get to know her grew stronger. I also wished greatly to read her poems, or hieroglyphs, as she called them. I yearned to make the poor girl my own, despite her shortcomings, if there were any.

I knew the situation wasn't of her making or doing, so I put it behind me. Brandoni may be of use here; during the dedication, I would be bold enough to beg an audience with him, so as to argue my case, and to set the Rose straight...

... as her nature intended.

The searching of her background information soon turned out well, and I was contacted by the Hopping Drake to meet him at the *Nest*. I finished up, ready for the next student to take over the shift. I climbed down the ladder, and Tarque went over to me, checking out my work.

'You're very good, Daye. I like your intricacies. The swirl-abouts give good contemplative reflection.'

'Or a serious bout of nausea,' I grinned, 'But thank you. I am pleased you appreciate my work.'

'Oh, but of course we do.'

'I was thinking of Rose the entire time, and her beauty is incorporated in the design,' I revealed.

'Very original. The sunbeam splatter works well with the imagery,' Tarque complimented.

'She is sunbeam splatter to me. I evoked this by demonstrating her beauty among the chaos. I think it is very effective.'

Tarque glanced at the wall, then back to me. 'I think she'd be very flattered at your depiction of her. Yet, you hardly know her.'

'All I know is that she's in trouble, mate, and I'm determined to help her,' I stated.

'Well, before you go out and play knight-in-armour,' Tarque offered, 'Want to go for a drink?'

'I've got an appointment with Drake, but you may join us.'

We set our kits down, ready for the next lot to take over the following shift. I had my fill of it, and felt reassured that I was doing the right thing in getting my Rose *away from the syndicate...*

... but it wasn't going to be easy; if I *was* to get her away from them, though, she would blossom into a sweet surprise...

... ready to take back to Oconnalow with me...

... so I dared!

Tarque and I went out of Sanstratten, toward the *Nest*. We wandered inside, and Tarque ordered drinks for us. I noticed Drake, sitting at a table with his associates. I caught his eye and nodded, with return acknowledgment, as he beckoned me to join him.

I found Tarque at the bar. 'I'm sitting over there with Drake. You can sit with us.'

'Wouldn't miss it for the world.'

'His contacts never let him down,' I smiled, walking to Drake's table.

He greeted me with a smile. 'Hello, Wendie. I have something for you.'

Oh? 'I cannot fathom what it may be,' I joked, rolling my eyes.

He handed me a folded parchment. My eyes widened, as I opened it up.

'This is a baptismal entry,' I cried.

'Yes. I had the record copied out by one of the floating legals of clerks in the next district over,' he said. 'It turns out she was baptised as an infant, but in a different locality, as to keep the event hidden from the grandparents.'

'Makes sense,' I lightly spoke, as I read the faint ledgers. I repeated the written name on the document, *Ambrossia Silardicus. Wow, what a pretty name.* I found it disgusting that her family had forcibly changed it to this Rachel *Whatsit.*

This item also confirms a suspicion that Rose was no Old Styler, but a good Christian girl who had been *intentionally* led astray. I could bring this up with that Vatican fellow, showing the actions of the syndicate against our society. It would justify the means of expulsion for them.

I put it aside for now, as Tarque came with the drink orders.

Taking a sip of red wine, I told Drake, 'A Vatican representative is coming to dedicate Sanstratten. I could show him this to forge our grievances against the syndicate.'

'I know,' Drake answered me. 'I was hoping to dig quickly to attain this find. It would swing the argument our way and would please any of the Pope's staff.'

I asked in hope. 'Can I keep this?'

Drake thought for a moment, then held his hand out. 'Considering how you students live, it would be better held in my offices. It will be safe. I can get another clerk to make a copy and swear upon it, etc, if need be.'

'Prudent,' I agreed.

'Bottoms up,' Tarque toasted, taking a good swig from his glass.

I drank my lot, as refreshing as it was. It came too fast, and I got hit with a buzz in the head. I paid no mind to it, as I was used to this, and shrugged it off.

Offbeat, I blurted out, 'So when can I get my Rose?'

'She's with her family, imprisoned at their home, in her silent room,' Drake said.

'If we could pass a note to her,' I suggested, as I looked out the window.

The bustling about was regular, but less hectic. I got up, out of curiosity, and scanned the streets from a window, just with the ambition of seeing Rose out there, somewhere.

'Daye,' Tarque called, 'She's not there. Come back.'

I suddenly had an idea. 'Maybe Drake could pose as a policemen, or Tarque and his friends could cause a melee in the square, and I or yourselves could get Rose away from *that* family.'

Drake sighed, 'It wouldn't work. We'd have a price on our heads and the grandparents would look everywhere for her. There would be no peace here.'

Damn! Why??!! I asked for another drink.

'Go get it yourself, Daye,' Tarque huffed.

I felt anguished my idea was shot to poopery! I got up to order another drink. The outdoor scene changed a bit and new faces popped up.

Suddenly, I saw Rose...

... or I thought I saw her.

Good God, let me out of here!

I dismissed the extra drink and rushed to Drake and Tarque. 'She's out there.'

'Duh, we know she is,' Tarque quipped aloud.

'No, I mean, now,' I hurried my speech. 'We must get her. It's now or we lose her.'

'We cannot let that happen,' Drake buzzed. 'Come here, Wendie. Let's go see what's happening outside.'

'I'll wait here,' Tarque mumbled, still sipping his drink.

'We need you,' Drake ordered. 'Be prepared for a rescue.'

'Great, we have work to do, and on top, we have to play supermen. Alright.' He got up, drunk his last for courage and followed us outside.

I looked about, my eyes full of anticipation. Then, I saw her surrounded, like a small flower smothered by gigantic hedge. It pained me to watch, as Drake and Tarque discussed a plan. They got a few locals to comply, and a few women willing to act as decoys in Rose's stead. Of course, Rose was a unique person and it would be foolish to mistake someone else for her...

... unless you were that blind, ignorant or completely misguided...

... unfortunately, the syndicate excelled at all three.

CHAPTER XIII

We walked out of the tavern; I made my stealthiest moves ever. I was not going to let this go, nor was I willing to leave empty handed. I hid at the back of the usual street crowd, like I did at the Old Styler service-thing. Drake and Tarque also hid behind some people, and with a great stretch of the imagination (*ouch!*), Drake approached the family in question.

Exhaling a quick breath and a prayer, Drake announced to them, 'We're looking for a young lady, matching the description of someone in their early twenties, short and resembling your charge.'

The odious grandmother, the Medusa, turned to him and retorted, 'What business do you have to do with *my* daughter?'

Drake, in his posing in mock-capacity of a constable, searched through a few small blank pages bound together in booklet form (that he used as a prop). 'Ummm, it says here that she actually belongs to a different family, whose paperwork confirms she belongs to them.'

More protests flew from the grandmother. 'She's ours. She's adopted. She is my daughter's child.'

'That does *not* mean she is your child,' Drake continued dryly. 'And not according to her real family.'

He then placed the booklet within his inner pockets...

... which was noticed by the Medusa, who cried, 'Let me see that!'

A scuffle occurred between them, when other people joined in to help Drake. He gave one of them the booklet, to keep it away from the Medusa. That person took it and ran to Drake's office with Mercurial wings.

I, meanwhile, stepped in closer to my target. Rose looked around, quite confused in the melee. I caught her eye, which she then nodded to me. She scampered her way toward me, quickly and quietly, while the scream-fest between Drake and the Medusa had escalated into an all-town riot. Poor Drake had flourished into fiery, violent argument, with the help of the townspeople.

'It is obvious she doesn't want to be with you,' he said to the Medusa.

'Begone with ye,' one participant shouted, giving a fist to one of the other family members.

The grandmother Medusa had had her fight, but persisted nonetheless.

Just as I was getting even closer to Rose…

… Tarque stood by, ready to receive *'the ball'*.

'Damn it Daye,' he muttered to himself, 'Hurry your ass up. We've no time for this.'

Silently, slowly...

... softly, softly...

... I was right next to her, and said, 'Hi. Now's your chance.'

I extended my hand out. She did not hesitate to grab it. I sent her to go to Tarque, who (with her in tow) made haste to our dorm room building. Huddled under his arms, they fled the scene together in passionate fury...

... in the furious moment to get out of there in a heartbeat.

We did not speak further, and figured I'd meet them back in the dorms. Drake, however, kept the horror-in-human-form busy. I didn't care by this time, and left in silence. Rose was away, and *that* family was ill-equipped to fend off angry townsfolk…

… and the crowd upon *them* grew to savage proportions.

Heading back, I ran into Sans-Brys...

... who asked, 'Did you get her?'

How did he know that??? My mouth opened in shock.

'Oh, don't worry. I knew you were after that poor Rose girl. I had noted Rose's recent seclusion by her family, so when they showed up in town, I arranged the locals for your convenience of sweeping her off her feet. I'm not just a mad body, you know. I am a romantic, too, on my days off,' he smiled, then got serious. 'They are a menace to our town, though. I know their type. I had an ancestor who was part of it, and got out swiftly. It is sad the way they go, *but it is of their own making.*'

My heart couldn't be gladder. *A natural model with a brain???* That was something to behold...

... and it was no wonder that they named this town after the original Sans-Brys, nearly a century ago...

... *family could either make or break you...*

... and I saw both ends of the stick!

Shaking his hand, I profusely thanked him.

'There's a place for her at the dorms. A small room, but it should do for the week until the Vatican envoy arrives. Now, hurry, hurry, before the grandmother gets wind of Rose's absence,' he ordered.

I thanked him again, and ran to the dorm building...

... to find Tarque and his roommates with Rose...

... talk about awkward!

'You're back. Good,' Tarque gasped, having run a mini get-away-from-evil-people marathon. 'We'll have to put her into another room. She cannot stay with us.'

I cried out, 'What?'

'That is to say, she's limited as to one of tender manners,' he explained.

Rose understood the playful prejudice. 'Oh, because I'm a girl?'

'There should be ladies' quarters upstairs,' Woodes-Hastings suggested.

My eyes widened, with blue most intense. 'No, I want her to stay with me!'

'Then, you can sew your wild oats, if the needle is big enough and the thread is plentiful... *elsewhere*,' Woodes-Hastings remarked hastily.

'You can't stay with your wee little girlfriend, mate,' Tudmond sneered.

'Yea, it wouldn't be fair on us,' Nay-Smith protested.

'We'd want you to share her,' Cateliffe smirked.

'Oh no you don't...,' I nearly wanted to punch him out.

Buckingham had a solution. 'Sans-Brys arranged for her to stay in the small box room in the hall. She can share it with Wendie, if she so chooses. Does that satisfy you?'

'For a week, yes,' I accepted. 'I saw Sans-Brys. Brandoni will be here then.'

'To sort out your little friend, no doubt,' Buckingham intoned.

'As well as do the dedication of Sanstratten,' Tarque finished his friend's thought. He looked at Rose. 'You have no belongings.'

Rose looked around at the manly balance of testosterone and order, if only slightly ruffled and manic.

'It's like an encampment in here,' she observed.

'Somehow, you are correct,' Tarque agreed. 'But this place is not for you... nor *soppy sorts who fall in love*.' He eyed me in particular with that last phrase.

I tried to keep my cool about me. I knew the jealousy factor was high, concern astronomical...

... we only just met and hardly knew one another...

... but the fun of getting to know one another will be greatly anticipated.

The process faltered when Wilset tittered about. 'And your little Irishman could join you, cos he wants you... *badly*.'

The rest of them collapsed in laughter, except Tarque and Buckingham, who (being slightly older) held more refrain than their younger counterparts.

I blushed and exited the room to find that box room everyone was talking about. I found it, but it was as small as described. Considering that we did not have much, it was good enough. It'll have to do for the moment. Yet, I was unsure if Rose would appreciate the close quartered contact...

... the concept of roughing it would verify the most interesting.

I returned to the main room to fetch her, and together, we went into Boxville.

She pondered aloud, 'Rather small, no?'

'It'll be fine for us into next week,' I answered.

'Why a week?'

'An emissary from the Vatican is coming to dedicate Sanstratten. You can help us with finishing touches, and possibly meet with him.'

More rosy questions. 'What does the Vatican have to do with me?'

I hesitated to offer the information I had regarding that parchment Drake showed me at the tavern...

... but I had to give it a go, and tell her the truth about herself.

'Rose, my dear,' I began, 'Or shall I call you *Ambrossia Silardicus*.'

'Why call me that?'

'That is your real name. A friend of mine had found a baptismal entry that proves your natural origins. It is stronger than your birth entry, as it ties you to the Church, which is run by the Vatican. You do wish to be reinstated as a Christian?'

Rose freaked out at this, but not too widely. The room was too compact for excessive emotions. She scurried for answers to those unanswered questions that plagued her for much of her young life, though it was apparent she was aware of her original birth name.

'Wow, I didn't think that was possible, but I was hoping this would happen,' she cried, hugging me.

'It is and shall be,' I beamed at her. 'In fact, the Pope has taken an interest in you because you could tell his representative what's been going on inside the syndicate and how they treated you. You possess information that an outsider would never be privy to, which could be the link that can destroy the syndicate's hold on Sanbrisi, once and for all.'

She stood, pie-eyed, wide mouthed, with all the dreams she once had, with all the reflective feelings written out in her hieroglyphics...

... i.e., her poetry.

'So, my time with *that* family was like an undercover assignment?'

I laughed, 'Quite likely. One of these days, I want to read your hieroglyphs, if you so be bolden to allow me.'

I shared a super-rich hug with her, and gave her irresistible cute-puppy looks...

... to which she gave in. 'Fine. You win. You may read my poems. I'm torn between loving you and hating myself. It is so frustrating for one to understand me.'

'I do, Ambrossia, I do,' I assured her.

With further commitment, she stated thus clearly, 'I want an abortion from the past.'

A workman came in at that moment, and filed a bed into a corner, and took some supplies out for relocation. It felt odd that the fellow appeared, just as I made a breakthrough with my girl.

'I so look forward to reading your crazy vibe-work,' I exclaimed.

'They're in the university scroll-rags,' she replied, 'And readily available to those interested parties.'

I'll have a look for them.'

I took her to the bed, and had a quick lie-down with her. I held her close, contemplating our potential future together...

... it may not be much, but it will be the week of a lifetime.

CHAPTER XIV

In the week that came, I had much on my mind...

... the Chapel decoration, and...

... Rose (or *Ambrossia*, to you and me).

Getting to know her was charming, but moving past her difficulties compared to a pigsty. She was calm and soothing on the outside, but her inner being was wrought with distress. By my very being, I attempted to relax her and inwardly reflect her stronger outer shell. She put up a front, which melted in my presence, *showing that she was not all she thought she was, or what she was told she was.* I assured her continually that she was a fine person and needed time to heal. I would give her time, no matter how long it took. I was very interested in her inner being, demonstrated in the works she had written…

… and, after sampling some of her writing, I seemed to have a better understanding of the senseless wasteland:

Grace foraging in the dark,
Shone a light for me to see
The error of my stupidity.
You've crossed the many thresholds of age,
Yet, you hardly entered its mansion.
I wish to engage in heartfelt stimulation with you,
Gently persuaded...
Fervently put through the ringer of acquired ways,
The hardship fettered, ensuing to nothing for days.
I so long to see the hair sparkling off your chest,
As you paint with feeling.
Yet others are drawing conclusions resulting in an art gallery,
Misconstrued and reeling.

I reread the poem and thought it very good. Full of emotion and inspiring, but she had a choking way of expression. I wondered of her feeling for me. A poem could say it all, yet could disguise one's will as such or another.

Rose came up to me and hugged me tight. I needn't have worried after all. Hugs were free, but here, laid a penchant behind the warm tug...

... so I accepted the offer and returned it, just the same.

There was no commitment between us, though I savagely thought of taking her back to Oconnalow with me, even for an improved life...

... and I believed she would like that.

I still had my mind on her restrained poem. 'So what's up in your verse?'

'Oh that,' she dismissed, 'It's just a spurt of consciousness.'

'Do you really see me as someone you wish to be with? You know we are up against a heaping toad-hole of madness, you know. I trust you are aware I plan to attain a Papal audience to see you sorted.'

Rose turned to me and cried, 'What? Do you know what my family will do if they found out?'

'Found out what,' I challenged, staring intensely at her. 'And what if they do? You're young like me, with a whole lifetime ahead of you. What are you afraid of, my girl?'

'Repercussions... I do not like being used as an instrument.'

I thought her musical reference rather sharp...

... and I used one of my own...

... as competition, hee-hee.

'Oh, but I wish to pluck up the courage of a harp and take you with me singing away with you.'

Yet, she snapped at me. 'Stop teasing me, you!'

'I wasn't teasing. I am most assuredly serious about my proposition to you.'

'Well, then. I apologise for being harsh in my attitude.'

'You are very defensive. I hope to bring that out of you, someday. For now, though, are you up for more painting?'

She paused quickly before deciding. 'I want to help, if I may, providing no one sees me going to Sanstratten.'

'I wouldn't allow it.' I got up from the bed. 'Let's go to Tarque and fill him in.'

We went to the other dorm room where Tarque and his friends held court, hanging out during a quiet spell.

'Rose wants to help us again,' I announced.

'Good,' Tarque said. 'We're expected at Sanstratten in the morning. There were many compliments about our work so far. We would welcome her contribution.'

The fellow returned to his card game.

'Fold,' Woodes-Hastings uttered.

Someone put out a card.

'Done,' Wilset smiled. 'I won.'

Tarque's body then folded in defeat. 'Damn.'

I sniggered at the group, as Rose and I left them to their sobrieties. I got Rose to read more of her poetry to me, as I fondled, kissed, and then fell asleep in her arms...

... together in harmony...

... and what a harmony it was.

The next day, as planned, we carried out the final touches of the paintwork of Sanstratten.   Everyone put in their all, and even Sans-Brys took time from his classes to join us. It made sense, as most of his students were working with us in the Chapel. It was prudent he took charge, thus.

Rose helped my work even more so, as colour upon colour was splashed like an insult to her miserly past. She, too, made astounding efforts to become a part of our cause in hand. The feeling of freedom from many years of oppression was rolled into a large blast of progressive creativity.

Eventually, days passed...

... our colourful work bespattered upon ourselves with delight...

... when soon...

... Sanstratten Chapel was alit with multicoloured spiritual glory to be proud of.

Tarque rubbed his square chin. 'His Holiness's emissary will find this a much needed curio, wouldn't he?

Sans-Brys waved his hand. 'Nonsense. I firmly believe he will find it a unique place to worship; a fitting tribute to our heritage abroad and a glory to God.'

'Well, I hope he doesn't mind the busyness of it all,' Tarque muttered.

Sans-Brys overheard the wry comment. 'Nothing in God's eyes is too busy.'

I strode the interior with Rose, admiring the sculpting, the painting; the varied accumulated tasks that screamed of love.

'I think it's eye-catching,' Rose observed.

'It catches the Spirit of Heaven to me,' I added.

'They must have voluminous art supplies there,' she tittered.

I put my arm around her, continuing our stroll. Tarque and his other colleagues also felt accomplished in their handiwork.

'The Emissary of the Pope will love this,' Woodes-Hastings beamed.

'If he doesn't catch a dizzy spell,' Wilset laughed.

Everyone looked at the walls of colour, storytelling, and heritage-pride, when Tarque exclaimed, 'Magnificent.'

Sans-Brys walked though the working crowd, who were too busy ogling over their energetic project, and informed Tarque, 'We're done here. You can go have a rest. Our Papal visitors will be here in the next day or so; we must lock up and preserve our work.'

The crowd was filing toward the exit at that point, and unto the street. I covered Rose with a discarded scarf from the afternoon's run. It had paint on it, but I felt it would be best for her protection. I looked around me, wondering if anyone from that Old Styler syndicate of her family would be watching...

... and I even furthermore hated to think if they had the opportunity to break into Sanstratten, and to deface what we all stood for.

No, no, no! I had to keep my head clear. None of that rubbish should be even considered. If that family was still looking for her, they'd do anything to breach the loins of progress...

... hers or anyone else's, for that matter.

In short, I concluded that covering up Rose in a tatty rag would be more suitable than her being covered up in admonishment...

... and so we went on.

A heavy lock was put on the main doors and the side doors were secured. A few students volunteered to guard the place, ensuring that our time was not wasted there, keeping Sanstratten from unruly by-standards...

... which, in no doubt, we knew where *that* may be.

We were invited to join in at the *Nest* for a celebratory drinks party. The cliques of close chums had formed around the multitude of tables there. Tarque sat with Rose and me.

'Pleased with yourselves, I trust,' he said to me, sipping his drink.

I stared at Rose. 'Yes, It is a relief we've finished the Chapel and Rose here had finally showed me her hieroglyphs.'

'Hieroglyphs,' Tarque repeated quizzically.

'My poems,' she barked loudly.

'Ah yes. My friend Buckingham made a reference to this in an earlier conversation,' Tarque replied, then whispered, 'He's read them, you know.'

'Really,' Rose beamed, happy to see *someone* read her works.

'Actually, I think he's here, if you excuse me,' Tarque got up, 'I'll go and bring him over.'

He left us to find his friend. Rose and I had a silly moment together when the Hopping Drake approached...

... and ejected, 'What say you?'

I took a sip of my drink. 'Nothing much.'

'You've got Rose safe and still with you I see.'

With worry, I asked, 'Is her family still out for blood?'

'They are searching within their own community right now, in case she had a friend among them,' he began.

'Not likely,' she growled, remembering the treatment she received from her peers.

'Well, they don't know that,' Drake soothed. 'There are many to choose from. It will keep them busy for now. You should be long gone before they find her, or worse, suspect us.'

I feared the worst. 'And what if they do?'

He retorted back, 'And what if they don't. Keep it up, Wendie. Your fellowship with your dearest was a well earned one.'

'Earned?'

'You put out for her,' Drake hinted.

I still wasn't sure what he meant...

... so he defined it for me. 'You went to that so-called service of theirs to find her, didn't you? Word came back to me.'

I hung my head down...

... duh!

I lifted my head back. 'I did.'

'So, you've earned your keep, your salt, your wherewithal. And you can keep the girl, too.'

What optimism he emitted!

Yet, I was sceptical. 'I don't know the where or the with, but I want her all!'

'And you shall have her,' Drake smiled at me, as Tarque returned with Buckingham to join us...

... and Buckingham was certainly a man who crossed a few thresholds of age, to quote Rose, but he was still 'one of us'.

'Hello,' I said, extending my hand.

'Well, hello to you, my dear Wendie,' Buckingham engaged in a handshake with me.

'And how is my dear Rose?'

'Fine,' she answered dryly.

'It is gratifying to meet an illustrious poet from the student rags.'

'More like rages,' I giggled.

'Rages, rags, or whatnot,' Buckingham quipped, 'It's all in the creativity. You've read her work too?'

'She shared her... *hieroglyphs* with me,' I admitted.

Buckingham's eyebrow fluttered, 'Hieroglyphs?'

'That's is what they're referred to in longhand,' Rose explained. 'I am a keen writer, and scribble stuff down as quickly as my brain can manufacture it.'

Buckingham encouraged his support. 'Good going, girl. I've only read the finished printed articles. You enjoying your time with us?'

'Much so, I am,' Rose said, 'Wendie's quite the gentleman.'

'As are we all,' he agreed. 'You plan to return to Oconnalow with him. He lives on a farm, you know.'

'It doesn't matter where I live, as long as it is not with *them*,' she emphasised, with last word punched out with contempt.

'Just remember my friend,' Buckingham advised Rose, 'The foundation of a home is not only marriage, but the blocks they built underneath to make it.'

It was getting late, and I had had enough of pomposity for one day. I wanted to take her back to the dorms to get her off her road trip down memory lane. I knew I would succeed, because as I looked at her, she winked, smiled and showed intended desire for me. The mini-Vatican Council would be upon us shortly, as we planned for the distinguished visitation.

CHAPTER XV

The illustrious day came on as a mild and overcast spell. A line of dignitaries hovered over the valley, making their way into the town of Sanbrisi. The party consisted of Brandoni, who would officiate as the Pope's representative, his second, DeRino, along with subordinates, lackeys and hangers-on, all curious about the newly decorated Sanstratten Chapel. They all knew the work was done by foreign exchange art students; the point being to draw out talent where there was, and to make much of it.

Winding their way down dry country lanes, a few horsemen in the Papal party stopped for relief and for a drink. A handy bottle of wine was reserved for the more important crew, while the lesser folk that came along had to make do with ale at the roadside taverns.

The trip seemed enduring to most, yet it was a worthy cause for the Church. Not only were they to dedicate Sanstratten for religious use, they were also called in to resolve the problematic issue of *that* family, running the Old Styler syndicate, and to handle its unwilling member, Rose. Brandoni was vividly aware of the circumstances of her situation, made clear from correspondence, and was set on putting it right. A meeting would be planned between myself and the lesser Holiness, with regards to Rose, once the ceremonies were completed.

Sans-Brys entered the Chapel to see to the condition of all the hard work put into it. All seemed safe, and our time's effort remained intact. Nothing was put out of place to complicate matters, and if there were, it would be a difficult test to correct it before the Papal stream arrived.

I awoke in the small box room, with Rose beside me. I was more than happy to see her through the most enduring time of her life. She breathed low and calm, as if nothing were to touch her pretty little face.

Not a matter (the world could offer) would displace the placidity of an emotion floating upon her lake. Her utter stillness had surprised me, as I knew her mind was as squeamish as a sick tummy with a bug. I thought her body would fidget just as wildly.

And when it came to blows, she took it cleanly. She got up and ran away...

... heading toward me...

... a lone boy from Oconnalow...

(... *but not lonely, as I had family there.*)

Her love for me shined on, and her yearning to be free was most touching, settling into her consciousness like a much-needed layer of warmth on a cold day. It was a fundamental human force to be free, even if you were in the lower orders. Whether you would get it or not, was another story. The sudden change of resolution was not very common, but to be relieved of incompatibility should be first and foremost in mind.

I got up, thinking and wondering if the Chapel's adornment was still there, in case *that* family pulled one over us, just to get back at Rose for spite. I would not put it past them, so time will tell on the day. It would bother me gravely if any tampering was persistent there. I spent much time on the work, like everybody else, and I would think that any foolery on *their* part would amount to nothing short of rape, AND possibly murder.

The sky was a lonely, cloudy dull grey sort, the type you can see in Ireland before it rains. I didn't know if it would, so I put on a warmer tunic and readied a cloak.

Rose soon opened her eyes and called out, 'Wendie?!'

I spun around, heading over to her. 'Yes, my dear?'

She reached out for me to hold her, which I did, in pure love.

'Rose, Rose, *Ambrossia*, Rose,' I chanted, rocking her gently.

She let out a small laugh, and felt comforted at the thought of a comforting, no-holds-barred cuddle. I felt like I was in an adorned chapel at prayer, with the feeling of coolness stretched abound me.

Then she asked, 'That fellow's coming today, isn't he?'

'Oh, Brandoni,' I replied, 'Yeah. He and a huge Papal host. I just hope I can get them to see me to discuss your cause. I trust you still want to be removed from your family... on a *permanent* basis, perhaps?'

'Yes, yes, I do. Wendie, I'm of age, anyway, though I look much younger. You know I'm not immature. There is no rhyme or reason why I should further put up with their incessant nonsense,' she boldly admitted.

She looked away for a moment. I lifted her chin to assure her. 'If I've to say something about it right now, I'd liberate you right at this moment.'

She was frantic, clutching straws nearly. 'But what else could we do???'

I paused to think. 'We could get married.'

The word struck her like a gong sound screaming through an otherwise silent valley...

...DUH!

'Stupid me, why didn't I think of that??!'

'Ye don't ask, hon, ye don't learn,' I teased.

'Learn what?'

'The ways and means of being in love, which I most certainly am.'

I gave her a kiss...

... then she asked, 'Would you take me back to your Ireland?'

'As my wife, or engaged at least, yes. You would be most welcome. After we shift the balance against the syndicate, the tide will turn; maybe they'll leave.'

'They won't give up without a fight,' she warned.

I continued my dream. 'We could return, and you can finally meet my family...'

I nearly fell over in petty slobbery of mind, but I noticed the sound of the word *family* clearly made her uneasy.

'Wendie,' she called out, steadying me upright again, dismissing her hesitation quickly. 'You could have hurt yourself.'

'Then the love splurge was worth it,' I smiled.

'So I will meet your people,' she reconfirmed.

'Sure. They don't bite. They are nothing like your guys, nor do we uphold the same values, assuming *that* family has any.'

She took the slight in good favour. 'So you're a Christian then.'

'Through and through. Possibly, even yourself, if we can get Brandoni to reinstate you back into the Church, where you belong. I know your present status was not of your choosing.'

'No, it wasn't. They are using me to nurture a lie, I believe.'

'And thus it seems. Their hold on you is pretty strong. We must weaken it, if we are to get going together as a concern.'

We hugged and carried on preparing for the day.

CHAPTER XVI

Later on, a fair whack of the populace had gathered at Sanstratten Chapel, awaiting Brandoni and his group. The glorious and the good, the lowly and hardworking all marvelled at the quirky art of Sanstratten, all done up by us foreign exchange art students. We were needed and wanted by the townsfolk to breathe uniqueness into their otherwise plain-jane Chapel...

... and what a uniqueness it was for them to see.

It was vivid, and colourful with imagination, on a monumental scale, paralysing time with God. Pastels filled the walls with Biblical meaning, and sculptures explained it all in three dimensions. Little quirks of design, unique to those who made them, stood out to share the Celtic-British culture they represented. Everyone was amazed at the accomplishments noted herein.

With the rest of my group, I entered Sanstratten hand in hand with Rose. Now that she was with me, and had wanted it so, I never had her out of my sight. I also never reverted to calling her Rachel, as it was a name *that* family used to deny her true identity as *Ambrossia Silardicus*. She didn't like the name Rachel, either, because she knew it made up a pretence about her...

... a pretence set upon her by *them*...

... specifically, the grandmother, the Medusa.

I took a space in our assigned front pew, with Rose sitting beside me. The rest of us filled in the rest, and took over another pew for themselves. They tittered to one another like little schoolboys, as townspeople, great and ordinary-classed filled in the other pews of the Chapel.   Rose was filled with excitement, as was I. It would be amusing to see what Brandoni had to say about all this.

Brandoni's party, with Sans-Brys, and other municipal leaders sat in ornamented seating by the altar. They all expressed their trinkets of office about their person, making them look just as splendid as Sanstratten…

… but we did not have to paint *them*.

A small choir of prepubescent boys were assembled across from the municipal officeholders, robed in a white outer shell, covering a pastel coloured tunic underneath. They sat in designated rows of wooden pews, ornately carved at the ends with little Celtic knot designs and patterned down to the floor.

The pieces of all the arduous planning had fallen into place. It was most intense an experience for me, as I had never been to an assemblage like this one back in Oconnalow. Our church was frequented by villagers and other nobodies in all walks of life, who bothered to turn up. No dignitaries nor mayoral heroes, just people; the simple common folk that made up our society, coming together in prayer and worship, with a bit of a tipple and munch at communion.

My heart pounded softly, but my nature was sat unrestrained. Chatter-boxing came through at all angles, where people's half-understood conversations reverberated within Sanstratten's walls. There was much anticipation, as most people gathered here had never seen a Papal dignitary before.

Soon, a bell was rung to call to order. Drake, who I just thought was 'one of us', turned out to be more than that. As a lead merchant, along with his partner Hamilton Tallis, he had put in much investment into this project. He thanked us all for coming to the Service of Dedication and then introduced Brandoni.

Brandoni was impressive in his scarlet Papal garb, that glittered with metallic trinkets of honour. He led the service, which was filled with devotion and song. Incense gathered in the air like a flying bird, then wiggled its way though an atmosphere of delight.

Brandoni was majestic, in a wild way. His prepossessing face spelled tough and his posture bore no fear of challenges. If there was a challenge to be had, he would play its opponent. Nothing intrigued me enough about him, such as to write home about, with the exception of the low octave emissions of pontificated Latin he made as he spoke. It sounded like mumbling to me, but as there were so many people present, it made for a more persuasive distraction.

Rose, sitting next to me, provided another ready distraction for me. I found it difficult to concentrate, being young and in love with her, as I was. But, I tried to listen anyway, and despite the slight inaudibility, I had caught a bit of this:

'This Chapel is the way of illuminating our presence in the world. It reflects the light of our faith and belief in the Almighty. It further reflects the unique individual spirituality of the people who shared a taste of their culture with us. Let those who had partook in the creation of such stunning beauty rise in acknowledgement.'

We all got up to the alter to receive praise, and a small token of appreciation the size of a brooch pin. Everyone applauded us, as we faced the townsfolk. It had been a most triumphal day for us...

... and then Sans-Brys had this to say:

'To every one in Sanbrisi, I thank you for your gratitude, forbearance, love, patience and tolerance. When this town was named in honour of my forebear, Sir Pym, nearly a century ago, it was for the support of arts and the beauty that comes from the arts. I am proud to continue his artistic vision, to serve and teach you, for the good of all, to serve God and Man in naturalistic beauty.'

Some sniggering went on in the audience at his last words, for everyone knew what *that* referred to.

Just as Sans-Brys returned to his seat, the doors of Sanstratten were violated by an unwanted enemy. From the flung-open doors emerged some members of the syndicate and *that* family, including the grandmother known to many as the Medusa. Gasping was heard from the many folk in the pews, as the mal-contented newcomers scanned the peripheries for their charge. Their unwelcome stance was felt throughout the Chapel, as if it was being raped, possibly to be further tormented by weaponry.

People murmured among themselves, asking *who the hell are these jerk-offs were, and why did they barge in on such a lavish and holy affair?*

It became apparent as to their purpose, when that Medusa of a grandmother had shrilled out, 'I am looking for my daughter Rachel. Where is she? I know she is here. I will not leave here until you surrender her over to me.'

A crack-whip answer had surfaced sarcastically. It was our friend, Woodes-Hastings. 'And what if we don't?!'

Cateliffe also contributed a volley of fire. 'Yeah, come out and make us, you succubus. We know what you really are.'

Tarque looked at him. 'Succubus?'

'Latin for prostitute,' Cateliffe explained, whispering, 'A female who lies with sleeping men. This Medusa's a demon, the family specialises in mattresses, and she's a bloody lying, fraudulent Old Styler by nature. I thought it would fit the bill.'

'Well, remember where we are,' Buckingham interjected.

'Doesn't matter anyway. We must defend the girl, at whatever verbal cost we must expend,' Cateliffe continued.

'Righty-ho,' Buckingham agreed.

Now, it was Nay-Smith's turn to have a go. 'Your time is at an end. We do not want you nor will we give up the girl. We like her just as she is... WITH US!'

The final part boomed out, as the audience clapped at my friend's defiant defence in favour of my Rose.

As the highest ranking personage present, Brandoni confronted the offensive individual. 'Who is this you are on about? Rachel? There is no one here by *that* name. You are welcome to join us, or begone ye cads, and leave us to our ceremonies. We have done nothing to disturb your community, take care not to make a fuss here.'

'When an Old Styler crosses paths with the outside world, it IS our business to retrieve him or her, in this case, her. Everyone in our community knows it is forbidden to mingle beyond our reach,' the Medusa insisted. 'I know the girl has been taking refuge among your art students.'

As the horror of horrors looked around, I tried desperately to hide my little flower from the poisonous ruckus that flowed around us...

... and so what if she was her granddaughter...

... she is MINE now; so there, ye hussy!

Meanwhile, the other syndicate members had a field day bumping into the ornamentation, knocking things over, splashing ink bombs on the skilfully painted walls, ruining several month's work. Sans-Brys put his head in his hands, as Brandoni comforted him. *This meant everything to me, months and months of effort and teaching,* Sans-Brys thought, *and they're making spillages upon meticulous works of grace.*

Rose couldn't hold out much longer, compelled to put an end to this on her own terms. I kept telling her to ignore them and remain still, yet, she felt like revealing herself...

... and jumped away from my protective shelter, to face the dreaded evil she ran away from.

'I am here, but I will not go with you,' she panted and blew herself down. 'I detest you deeply, and I do not care if you are my mother's family. I do not care thus, if I am hastily related to you through that adoption you rigged. I do not enjoy being subject to your fraudulence, nor do I like being bullied by the Old Styler ways you uphold. I will no longer have it. I hate you, and never will return to you or your fold.'

The Medusa lunged toward her, grabbing her arm. 'You are to come with us right now. You are under punishment, because you did a bad thing today. What you said is equally rotten.'

Rose was puzzled. 'What? That I told the truth about *your* family? To defend myself before these goodly people? To help create something beautiful and to diminish your so-called superiority over me?

'I believe this is what I want to have, and to be. Your ways mean nothing to me, absolutely nothing.'

The Medusa had a ready answer, hissing as always. 'So, you would rather be in a church, with the rest of this tripe? You find yourself comforted among strangers? *They do not care a scrap about you.* Nobody does but us. We have done much for you, and want to continue doing so. I know you do not like us, and that you think I'm a bad mother. But you are ours to pursue. *You are forever part of our family; you will follow our ways. We will never let go of you; you are an Old Styler, once and for all.*'

Tarque bit his lip and eagerly wanted to punch the lights out of her...

...but had this to say instead…

(*…and with what force to reckon with!*)

'She does not want to come with you. You can goad her, bully her, and force her all you want. You think you've done much for her, as you stated, but look at her now. She is terrified of you. Her mind has gone afar. She has progressed beyond your Old Styler ways, just like those people of old, who got the Divine Message. She will never respond to you.'

'Well, what do you know anyway, you NOSser,' came the obvious snide-mannered comment.

The tension in Sanstratten was too much to bear. By this time, Rose had returned to her place next to me, and never laid eyes away from the material of my cloak.

Drake shouted out. 'You took her by force, and without choice. No, she's not one of yours. I have proof here that so states.'

Brandoni whispered to Drake. 'Can I see it?'

'It is her baptismal entry, proving they took her wrongly into their Old Styler religion. Hold it in your cassock, your Grace,' Drake suggested, handing him the document. 'We don't want *that* piece of evil getting a hold of this.'

'You can always get another copy,' Brandoni waved his hand, as he hurriedly took the parchment into his possession with the other, without a glance. 'I'll get a clerk on it, if you need it.'

'Thanks,' Drake still spoke, and took his seat. 'This record means she *is* of the Church. This was a legitimate event and so stands, as this girl's wishes are revealing contrary to that of the grandmother. There were witnesses.'

'I know, I put them there. Alright, they were not familial, but for anyone who attends, it counts as ordered.' Brandoni then faced the parley. 'I now say unto you again, you could join us, or leave. As you've proved to be hostile to us and your intention, to be disruptive, I order you to leave immediately. We wish to rid ourselves of your disgraceful conduct.'

'I will not leave without my daughter,' the Medusa protested, still holding her own...

... her own what, I could not say...

... nor wish to think upon.

Brandoni further questioned the menace. 'Had you thought about a reward, or incentive to give to her, if she yields to your demands? Had you given her a choice, by which she could decide to live by?'

There was no answer. The bats in the belfry just flapped their wings, and flew out of the open window in their minds.

Brandoni realised the direness of the situation. 'Oh, so you did not give her a choice, incentive, or reward.'

Then came a smart-mouthed answer from another family syndicate member. 'Why should we? She's a very badly behaved young lady, in doing what was wrong to begin with. Despite her rejection, she is still one of us.'

'Not according to this document I have here,' Brandoni patted his breast, where the proving parchment was hidden. His sternness continued. 'She does not want to be with you. There is nothing you can do to make her. She is young, *but not young enough to be led on by you anymore.*'

The intensity of the moment heated up to maximum, as the Medusa blurted out blindly, 'I will give you three seconds to surrender Rachel to us.'

A loud voice overcame the din. 'She will not go!'

It was little ol' me, the sweet, succulent Timoseph Wendel Daye, of Oconnalow, Ireland, ready to do battle with this highly-strung monster.

And this was my confronting verse of crowning glory:

'Your claim upon *your* 'Rachel' is unfounded and invalid. *She has the right of choice, and her choice is to be with me,*' I growled back at her viciously. 'Your face spells psycho, but you cannot spell it right. She is not keen on your sharp focused vomit offerings, because I know. *I was there.*

'I covertly attended your trifling Old Styler ceremony, and it sucketh wads of gunpowder (in my opinion), which you do not need to import! You use it to entrap, and it's a trap for her that she does not want to continue in. She is a delightful being, warm and kind. You are suffocating a wondrous spirit. You are in league with the damned.'

I paused, exhaling, knowing there was a bit more I wanted to strike with, using a word the Medusa said earlier, re-imagined to fit my quip. 'Where I come from, OSSer rhymes with tosser, which is what you lot are!'

Thunderous applause exploded, as I sat back down, my piece being spent well.

Tarque patted me on the shoulder. 'Well done, Daye.'

'Thank you,' Rose gave me a kiss on the cheek.

Sans-Brys made a formal statement and complaint. I can see the pained look of disgust and regret upon his face, as he was about to share a more naked side of himself…

… it scared me into a latrine…

… and it was a most long-winded dossier I could ever imagine. 'I don't like discussing this, but I fear this must be said. Over a millennia ago, I had an ancestor, who came from an Old Styler background, which was called something else at that time. He lived in the Roman province of Mentis, the land between two continents. He had a similar dispute with his family, not unlike yourselves with your Rachel. Yet, their difference was in opinion of profession.

'Through the backbone of history, he came to redefine himself, later relocating to Gaul (now France), and then a few centuries ago, his descendant relocated to Britain and had made a life there. Then, the aforementioned Sir Pym arrived here in Italy from Britain, later having this township so named in his honour. Thus, all members of our Sans-Brys clan had made something of ourselves, moving on from familial squabbles and petty soul thievery, to something that is more in line with spiritual and social prowess. I must say that you Germanic insurgents are an insult to the ancient people of *that faith*, which date back to Biblical times. You think you could go *that* far back in your own histories, but realise that you've only just joined the club. How you got into it, is unknown, which is just as bad. In your case, I am aware of the fraudulent nature of your beliefs, and I firmly believe that you are using poor Rose to cover for your activities. It is a shame that I state this, but I think your kind must be eradicated, and with utmost prejudice.'

More agreements, wider murmurings flew on, as Drake came up to speak. 'Your so-called mattresses are putting our township to sleep, while you have taken over. You think you scored big all these years, but you lost some points along the way.'

The tide turned against the Old Styler syndicate, but the Medusa had the last word.

'Have your freedom, have your choices. You think you know better than us, but you do not. Well, I do not care for your thoughts nor your opinions. The hell with you and be damned.'

She walked out the door, empty handed (i.e., *without Rachel, ha-ha*); the head was held high, and the being was not dejected. Her followers wandered behind her, showing a similar blasé attitude about them.

Now *this* was something one would never ever say aloud...

... especially in church...

... and most certainly not in front of the Papal Emissary that was Brandoni.

Brandoni gave a nod to his second, DeRino, who got up and left Sanstratten though a side door at the rear. He stealthily leaned against the Chapel building, hiding from view until he was ready. He saw the syndicate go its merry way...

... and sought out the opportunity, too good to miss.

So, like Perseus of old, and Carmikulus of another story, DeRino drew his sword...

... grabbed the grandmother...

... and destroyed the monster that she was.

Some onlookers watched from the inside, then ran to tell Brandoni the deed was done. The Papal man smiled, knowing this was the only way to free Sanbrisi from the terror of the Old Styler syndicate...

... as well as preserving the admiration, and cosmos of Sanstratten Chapel, despite the incredible interruption she suffered.

Sanstratten, thus remained intact, and the beauty we laboured on, had a resonance that shone with strength. If the Chapel was a real woman, I would liken her to Rose, as she, too, had been 'raped' by the injustice that was the Old Styler syndicate.

Brandoni went outside, and called out to the straggling Medusa party. 'I give you physical expulsion with cruel imposition. You are no longer free to remain in Sanbrisi. Return to where you came from, or you will suffer the same fate as the grandmother.'

Like rats in a nest, the stragglers scurried back to their respective places, careful not to trip over the Medusa's corpse, and in a few moment's time...

... the entire syndicate had left the building...

... *permanently.*

The citizens of Sanbrisi rejoiced at the syndicate's fall and hosted celebrations and block parties which lasted for hours...

... however, despite the hatred against *that* family, the concept of a mattress sounded like a good one, and a local manufacturer, one Michael D'Angelo took it up as a growing concern. He bought out the stock left behind by the syndicate, and opened up a shop on the Via Valastra called *Sistina's Bedcover.*

My friends and I were relieved at Brandoni's expulsive order, and Rose was now free to follow her heart to me. I kissed her, and sought out Drake to see about meeting up with Brandoni.

'Just the fellow I've been looking for,' Drake smiled, as he beckoned Rose and I to attain that audience we needed with the Papal Emissary.

CHAPTER XVII

I was led to a smaller room within Sanstratten Chapel. Brandoni and DeRino were sitting there, still looking resplendent in their apparel, awaiting our meeting. The low octave emissions from Brandoni were predominant, as he was in conversation with his deputy. They didn't look up at us, nor did they think to remove their clothing to make themselves more comfortable. It was as if their comfort was in their formality.

Drake, Rose and I stood in front of the Papal duo, waiting for them to speak to us. They kept us detained a few moments, as they discussed important matters...

... such as finding a good place to eat, or setting high upon an incorrect sock colour scheme...

... my mind played dirty like that.

Drake broke the stalemate with a throat clearance, and the duo then marked us for attention.

Brandoni began to speak, finally getting to meet the young girl he earlier defended. 'So this is the young lady from the Old Styler community you bring before me?'

'We refer to them as the syndicate, but yes, this is she,' Drake asserted. 'It was not of her choice that her family had caused grief to herself and *our* communities in Sanbrisi. Much of their activities happened before this girl was even born, so she had no part in its making. She certainly did not continue their wishes, which made them distrust her, I believe. We cannot control to whom we are born to, can we?'

'No, we cannot,' Brandoni agreed, then looked at Rose. 'Approach, young lady. Rose, is it?'

Brandoni took out the parchment upon which this meeting was hinged.

'Ah, *Ambrossia Silardicus*, then,' the Emissary continued, now having checked it to see what the fuss was about. 'You want to return to the Faith of the Church?'

As if she was getting married, Rose replied, 'Yes, I do. I confess I do not know much about it, but I know the Old Styler ways did not agree with me, and never had.'

'Doesn't agree with society, either,' DeRino interjected quickly.

'Quite, quite,' Brandoni concurred. 'Ambrossia, you are a unique girl, and have friends who really care about you, possibly more so than your family. Don't worry about your mastery of our Faith. You will get there in time, but you need to commit to it, in order to do so.'

He then read more prayers in his pontificated Latin, having Rose kneel and reaffirm her beliefs, i.e. concerning her commitment to the Church and faith in Christ, like a confirmation.

She smiled at this and nodded in agreement.

Brandoni excused DeRino out for a moment. He went off to the back and returned with a bucket full of water.

I was pissing myself with intense curiosity. 'What's the bucket for, then?'

'This is for your little friend, Ambrossia,' Brandoni answered.

He then chanted more pontificated Latin over the girl. *This was nearly like witnessing an exorcism!* He signalled DeRino for that bucket, then (once obtained) poured the contents over Rose's head...

... emptying the vessel; its contents dripping all over her body.

Rose was shivering with shock, when Brandoni had DeRino fetch a towel from the vestry and dried her off.

'What was that all about? I thought that document was enough to convince you I was part of your faith all along,' Rose cried out.

'But, would it convince *you*? This is to reinstate you to the Faith *again, and for all time*. You've reaffirmed your vows and got a baptism that you are fully aware of, present for, and one that I know you will never, ever forget. After what you'd been through, I have assured that you will never be led astray again. *Ambrossia Silardicus*, daughter of Joseph Silardicus and Susan *Whats-her-name*, you have been restored and welcomed in your return to the Church and *let no one ever rend you asunder from your precious faith again*.'

'Congratulations,' DeRino concluded. 'It is done. They are finished.'

Brandoni added, 'The syndicate has been banished from our Italian shores and the Medusa is dead. You are free to pursue who and what you want, *Ambrossia Silardicus*.'

Rose shook hands with the Emissary and his deputy. She then gave me a hug and shook hands with Drake.

Brandoni further asked us, 'Is there anything else we can do for you?'

My mind raced to an earlier chat I had with Rose about marriage. Maybe this fellow could help us with that...

I piped up, 'How about marriage, then?'

'Marriage?' Brandoni's eyebrow raised. 'Marriage? I cannot get married, you know and DeRino's taken his vows, too.'

I knew he was joking with us; I never figured on a papal fellow to bestow humour, while in formal capacity.

Drake clarified, 'Could you wed these young people, Wendie and Rose?'

'Ah, yes,' Brandoni let out a short cough. 'Very well. I trust you'd want a meaningful ceremony. Perhaps in this Chapel, that you'd worked so hard on to make beautiful.'

'I want to be legally and spiritually bound to Rose,' I begged. 'No one shall rend us apart.'

'No one will dare try,' Brandoni said, 'I had scattered them about, remember. I'll get you two bound, one way or other.'

Rose and I joined hands, and yelped for joy. It would be the first step of another commitment, a lasting commitment...

... together.

I reflected upon a full scale marriage at Sanstratten, which would be one of the first main events to take place there. Yet, I remembered my family back in Ireland, and realised they would not be here…

... and I told this to Drake.

He then replied, 'If they love you, they'll understand, son. Besides they wanted you to *grow up*, didn't they?'

I couldn't pose an argument to that one, and left it alone. I still felt homesick, but wild about Rose, at least. I was not happy about my folks unable to attend our ceremony, but there were many other people who would make up for their absence.

We thanked Brandoni and DeRino for their help, and allowed them to officiate at our wedding. After the formalities, Rose, Drake and I left the Chapel.

Rose gave me a big hug, and shook hands with Drake, thanking him for all his help.

'No problem,' he smiled, 'No one should come between you now. The grandmother had been killed and the family/syndicate had fled. Sanbrisi has had no further interruptions from them, nor anything regarding the Old Styler ways.'

'After the wedding, I want to return home,' I stated. 'There's nothing for me here anymore, and Rose will be better off in Oconnalow.'

'I'll see what I can do for you,' Drake suggested.

Rose asked me, 'What's Oconnalow like?'

'Oh,' I reflected, 'It has a natural green beauty, with plants, flowers, animals in the fields, family, faith, and friendly people. You'll blossom there.'

She hesitated at the word 'family', *again*. 'Your family?'

'They're all right when you get to know them. They'd be happy to meet you. There is nothing untoward about them. They are simple farm folk, with their own ways about them. My dad, especially. He's a real card-in-the-deck, if you know my meaning.

She giggled. 'I think I understand. I'd like to meet him. He sounds inspiring.'

'And Mother's a great cook. She puts sense into eating.'

Rose smiled at me with affection. I put my arm around her, as we headed to the *Nest*, where the three of us sat down for a drink.

CHAPTER XVIII

Preparations for our marriage were in their fullest. Tarque's group of friends helped ready Sanstratten for the fateful day. The town murmured in excitement, seeing their new Chapel being put to good use.

Brandoni stayed around with DeRino, as he promised to officiate the event. Sans-Brys sent us a small note of thanks and congrats, saying that he'd be there to see us off into our new lives. He continued in his artistic professorship and taught new pupils of art. He also considered retirement for a rainy day, when he befriended someone with a flashy vision describing the glories of flying machines. Whether Sans-Brys agreed with it, was another matter entirely.

Most of us were rushing about, many sorting things out for us, while Rose and I got fitted into our wedding gear. All and all, it had been worth it to remain in Sanbrisi, and not to haste back home. Autumn winds cooled things down a bit, but the weather was not extreme, to say the least. The town quieted down somewhat, since the storm of the Old Styler syndicate had dissipated; its members fleeing to other areas of choice...

... as long as they were far away from us.

A sigh of relief of the township was felt all over. The syndicate left a gruesome memory on the people, and it took some time for them to move on from its horrific damage. Businessmen who were affected, had to work twice as hard to regain their pre-syndicate glories. Churches and chapels, including Sanstratten, were packed full with continuous, fervent prayers for recovery and thanksgiving toward that young lady who partook in *that* family's downfall (leading to the syndicate's departure)...

... and it was that young lady I was about to marry...

... though *her* time of recovery I reckoned would take much longer to cover.

Soon enough, on a Saturday in late November, we were about to change our very lives. Sanstratten Chapel looked as good as on Dedication Day. The sculptures that had been damaged during the intrusion of the syndicate, had been restored and returned to their original places. Murals damaged from the ink bombs were repainted and filled in. Flowers and silk streamers flowed through the sanctuary, and the invited townsfolk eagerly entered the Chapel to enjoy the special occasion.

I awaited my Rose, as I stood at the threshold of the altar, ready to make sacrifice of my youth, only to now become a man. I had Tarque as my best man, and it was arranged that Drake would walk Rose down the aisle.

Music played from (what I thought was) a grandiose organ, as Rose, Drake and a few bridesmaids came through the door. It was a welcome arrival, unlike the previous time that somebody went through the door of Sanstratten to cause a brutal scene.

Despite all that foul-plated history, Rose looked stunning in her beige-bodice lace dress, looking like heavy cream in warm summer sunshine, in spite of the season. I looked plain in comparison, but a simple, well-fitted fanciful tunic was enough for me...

... even though it had silken drawer lining and wallpaper style patterning.

Rose took her rightful place besides me on the dais. Brandoni then approached us. After the preliminary bits were spoken, the main line of questioning began, just like at that meeting she and I had with him.

'Do you, Timoseph Wendel Daye, take unto thee, *Ambrossia Silardicus*, to be your lawfully wedded wife?'

Without hesitation, I claimed the fateful answer. 'I do.'

'And you, *Ambrossia Silardicus*, take unto thee, Timoseph Wendel Daye, to be your lawfully wedded husband?'

Likewise, freed out of a bitter nightmare, came, 'I do.'

I then placed the ring on Rose's finger, to symbolise our forever love, and defining friendship.

'I now pronounce you man and wife,' Brandoni concluded. 'Wendie, you know what to do.'

'I certainly do,' I smiled, lifting that accursèd veil. I gave her the kiss of her life. We melded as one, as the verbiage stated, and it felt fantastic to have accomplished such a holy experience...

... without *that* abusive, evil family barging in to cause refuse on the proceedings.

'God, we've made it,' Rose cried out deliberately.

'Not only had you been restored to the Church and birthright, but to me, to me, Ahhh,' I shouted back to her.

We hugged in front of the gaping masses, who thunderously applauded, as if they'd seen an award-winning theatrical performance...

... but this was no acting job...

... this was very real indeed...

... and I meant every word of it!

Once we left Sanstratten, we had a small party at the *Nest*. It was an all out, way out bit of the social, yet it was high time I thought about home...

... and asked Drake about the next ship back.

'I can arrange for you to board the *Rafferty O'Brien* again and sail around Spain, or you can go by land, going north and through France and get a packet to Ireland from Brittany. I guess you are eager to get home to your family,' he said.

I smiled. 'That I am, and to introduce them to my wife.'

'You just want to fulfil the rites at Oconnalow.'

Rose looked at me strangely.

'I'll explain later,' I assured her. To Drake, I asked, 'How did you know of our rituals?'

'It's legend, son. Legend... and I am into legends,' came his reply.

The party continued long into the night.

CHAPTER XIX

Early winter sea storms prevented our passage away from departure, and Drake suggested we spent Christmas in Sansbrisi. He had business to attend to, but I took him up on the offer anyway, and I thought it would be a good opportunity to share with Rose a memorable Yuletide. The weather in Sanbrisi itself was far from recognisable, compared to that in Ireland. Untypical warm weather (to me) lit the seasonal skies with comfort and assurance.

I gave much affection to Rose, but saved her for the rites at Oconnalow. There was more than *one* way to pleasure the lass. The sweet air of relief never left me, since the Old Styler syndicate and *that* family left Sanbrisi. Being with Rose was a marvel, as she blossomed into the person *she* was entitled to be, as I expected she would. She was far from the staid, restrained and plain girl I first met at the well, so long ago by now.

Tarque and his friends invited us for Midnight Mass at Sanstratten. It was a topical idea, and a good introduction to Rose to our more beautiful way of living. The Chapel was alit with eager parishioners, awaiting the final moments of Midnight, when everyone could loudly exclaim *Buon Natale* (Merry Christmas) to one another. In the corner of the Chapel lay a curious, and elaborately decorated *presepi*, which depicted the Nativity scene. This tradition dated over a hundred years ago to St Francis, who put together an ensemble to re-enact the Birth, and held mass in celebration.

The *presepi* at Sanstratten was daring. The animals were made artificially, by the Artist's Society of the University of Sanbrisi; some of the students there having worked on the Chapel. Real people dressed up in costume to fill out the human roles, and a few did so in turns, like a shift pattern. This was a special tradition in Sanbrisi, as the townsfolk all took part in this in some portion of their lives. Most of them played the Infant child, and there was not one person there who could state otherwise.

This made the people more fervent and faithful to their religion. It was no wonder their clash with the Germanic Old Styler invaders was so traumatic for them.

With candles and glorious musical refrain, I knew Rose would be in for a treat. I later asked her if she was coping with all this newness around her…

… and her reply was, 'Quite triumphantly, actually. I am fine with this, as this is the Truth.'

I gave her an affirming squeeze to her hand. *Atta girl, your destiny is complete!*

Now that she has been sorted out in the brash, wild way that Brandoni handled her, I figured she would do all right in the end.

After an awe-filled service, we returned to the dorm with the others. Rose and I went straight to bed, while Tarque and his pals had riotously teased one another with seasonal larks, sparks and japes, as well as opening an odd present.

However, the next morning, being Christmas, we would not get away without a festive laugh or two…

… as a knock came upon our daytime clearance.

'Wendie, are you awake?'

I was too stumbled as to identify who it was, but I answered anyway. 'We'll join you shortly.'

Footsteps went away, when I stirred Rose's pot awake with a caress on the cheek and a kiss.

She answered. 'Wendie?'

'My love, Merry Christmas.'

'Merry Christmas to you, too.'

I got up to the dresser and turned to smile at her. I then threw a tunic at her with practicality.

'Get up. The gang's waiting for us.'

She and I got dressed and we went out of our small boxed hideaway. The others in the main dorm shouted seasonal compliments and greetings as we entered their portal. We exchanged hugs and handshakes, as that was all that most of us could afford…

… no matter, it was the thought that counted…

… and *this* company was a gift enough, as it was.

Tarque rubbed his hands with glee, like the true inner schoolboy that he was. 'Ready for a good smash up at the *Nest?*'

A voice cried out. 'What about morning Mass?'

'Never mind that,' Tarque snapped. 'We've already been last night, and I am getting hungry.'

'I second,' Woodes-Hastings concurred.

And with that, we went to the *Nest*. Walking through town was not difficult, for the bustle of people who would have been out, are all at home; bustling about in their own kitchens and rooms in celebration. All was quiet on Sanbrisi's front. Not a store was open, not even a small shop. The taverns were all shut, but for our beloved *Nest*, which stayed open after a small bout of internal wrangling over holiday hours, between the proprietor/cook, Robin Sully and his assistant, Jack Ritts (who were British/Celts, like ourselves). It seemed absurd to do so, but they concluded that there may be wanderers who had no where to go, or no family to turn to, on this important day…

… and there would be no competition to threaten a possibly *lively* business…

… as there *were* always lone students about, in need of a quiet and quick buzz.

I was grateful to spend the holidays here, and to hasten to remain in Italy. Yet, I missed my family, especially now at *this* time. Sadness came upon me, as word of the storms brewed and overturned intention as fast as the storms themselves would overturn ships. At least I got to spend more time here with Rose, in such a dramatic a place with customs sharing equal drama. I did hope that the storms will calm down eventually, so we can return home soon.

There was a handful of patrons at the *Nest*, as expected. There, Sully and Ritts tended to their needs with food and drink, in return for previous time's labour. The place was lavishly decorated with green and candlelight (separated, with due care). The notable *presepi* basked in the centre, done again by our fellow art students (who also worked on Sanstratten), now sitting and drinking, here with the rest of us today.

All who came to the *Nest* during the past week, had marvelled at its detail and colourful elaboration. Everyone contributed their talent, time and effort, and some of these students took jobs at the *Nest* for the harried season, in exchange for meals. We were down to our last few coins, so, we too had pitched in there. Tarque gave Sully a small donation and his friends, to help out where needed.

The food was exquisite, nearly rivalling Mother's always-delicious meals. We had fried, chopped eels, pasta-adorned soup, a variety of meats, such as beef and pork, some vegetables and a large *panettone*, which was a cake with nuts and fruits, laced with a little booze, to give it more flavour.

It was a good meal, and even Rose enjoyed it. She never complained once, nor disrespected *our* ways, knowing how she was raised was *totally bogus*. We all spruced up the place afterwards, now that the penny was upon us to work. We washed the pans, crockery and utensils, cleaned tables, and served customers consisting of those lone students and passers-by in the street, itching for good heartiness of the season. The bit of singing later on, added to the craziness of the ambience. The experience gave us further proximity but not too close toward discomfort.

We had a fantastic time, being with good friends, food, and frolic, as well as a touch of work. It made for a most merry duration, and excitement was had by all. We thanked Sully and Ritts for their endless hospitality, as they thanked us for our free labour. To me, *that* was what a true Christmas was all about...

... and it even taught Rose a thing or two about how the *real* world works.

CHAPTER XX

At very last in the this new year of 1392, I was now able to secure transport for myself and Rose to return home to Oconnalow; the early winter storms having abated. As suggested by Drake, we first had to go by land, up northward, then west through France. We would board a packet at St Malo, in Brittany, sailing westward into the Atlantic, toward the Irish coast, terminating in harbour of Queens-Cobhayr. The sea crossing would possibly be most deadly, if newer storms broke out and the crew were not cerebrally alit with knowledge of those waters.

However, crazy notions and fear never stopped the sea merchants from their trading...

... and so we hastened onward.

To the goodness of my heart, we were not to be alone on this trip. Drake accompanied us, as he had business at Queens-Cobhayr. Tarque and his friends from the dorm had completed their term in Sanbrisi and also intended on going home to England. They thought they had enough culture to serve one lifetime. They also missed their families. Even Wilset made up his mind to return, even though he wanted to be more cultured...

... he decided to leave it for the artisans and budding scientists who became more prominent when we left...

... but he did admit to us that he had a grand time of experience.

So everyone packed it in, contributing funds toward the journey, and ride out of Sanbrisi forever...

... leaving behind Sans-Brys, whom we loved, and who wished us a safe journey home...

... the beautiful Italian weather we were so blessed with...

... and most fortunately, the negative ravages of the syndicate that we all damned wholeheartedly, with the exception of Rose (who we knew wasn't at fault).

And so, we all departed Sanbrisi by carriage, and we did enjoy the venture out. The creation of the look of Sanstratten Chapel had all been worth it. Those who since visited, either for worship or pleasure (i.e., looking at the murals, etc.), marvelled at our artistry and detailed interpretation of our native culture. It was an amalgamation of triumph and beauty. Some returned for a second look, while others went in daily for their personal vigils.

The road ahead was a long one, and I certainly saw no end to it, not knowing the duration. What I did know was that the long haul would weigh down on us all. I didn't know whether it was quicker to go by sea, but to travel around Spain caught me a little off-kilter. I cannot recall how I got to Sanbrisi in the first place, as it all had been a blur to me by this point. All I remember was that slanty-eyed Sandy fellow who gave a toss enough to speak to me, as well as the endless work aboard that took the mind off time.

And the out-of-town dirt roads were not paved with silk either...

... they weren't paved at all!

So, we took the more regulated Roman roads out, because they had better upkeep. It was a long hard trip, and when we finally crossed into France, I sensed we were inching closer to home.

Rose took it all well and put up with us keenly, reading aloud to us the hieroglyphic poems she brought along for the journey, which she salvaged from her former home. She'd never travelled crazy-long like this before.

I also considered (once home) of having a burn-up of my clothing, and put on some freshly-woven Irish linen on me. I'd have Rose do the same...

... after a cool dip in the stream, cleaning the crap and such off our stinging bodies.

After a week or so, negotiating through the fair-old, chunky size of France, we all soon parted company at St Malo. Tarque and his bunch all wished us the best and boarded their vessel for England, while Drake, Rose and I boarded a packet bound for Ireland.

It was unusually mild weather, and the normally raging sea had become calm. The seaman and navigators took full advantage of this and made sail immediately. There was no hesitation, with the attitude of *just go!*

With a sudden interested wind inside me, my feelings for her and home were surrounded in vast swathes of thought:

The ejaculatory madness that envelopes us,
Gave way to the execution of charms.
As the sun shone down on my face,
I've become delirious with agitation over you.
I see a complete debauchery of a luxury item,
Itching to go below the ol' homestead,
With the ravishing pulsar of my being.

It was hard for me to believe I could be a poet, but there was a knack for the budding wordsmith in this here farm boy. Rose complimented me on my effort and thanked me for the kind sentiment.

We coasted on, through the waters...

... Rose was getting really tired...

... and I was still dreaming about having that heavenly bath in the stream with her.

Another week went by and smile on my face widened when the familiar harbour lights shone out from a distance, even in daylight, as there was a fog about when we arrived. The sailors moved the ship in line with the approach, and we docked safely at Queens-Cobhayr...

... with my sister and father waiting for me...

... and I knew I would have much explaining to do...

... after Mother's home-cooked meal.

I ran up to them and embraced them with a hug I never thought I would give them…

… a good *manly* hug.

Rose stayed beside me, but remained shy and silent, letting us get on with our reunion.

Jaice asked me, 'So, Wendie, how did it go? We were so worried about you, but I guessed you were spending time *growing up*.'

I took her coarse remark with a pinch. 'I don't know where to start. There was so much. I went to the dock, like you told me to, then helped load cargo aboard a ship called the *Rafferty O'Brien*, got paid for it, got lopped on the head, then ended up in Italy of all places!'

Father continued, 'What did you do in Italy, son?'

'Enrolled in an art school; I was sponsored by a fellow called Drake, whose partner is called Tallis, whose twin works at our dockside.'

'William Tallis?'

'That's him. Then I ended up helping out to paint a newly built chapel called Sanstratten with other British kids. It turned out sensational. I wish you could've see my work.'

'Yeah, I would have liked that.' Father eyed me sharply, then saw the girl beside me. 'And who is this young lady?'

I took Rose by the hand. I exhaled pretty sharply, as I introduced her to her *new* family.

'Father, Jaice, I want you to meet my wife, *Ambrossia Silardicus Daye*.'

Things went uncertain, and the shock of my marital status took Father by surprise and joy. Jaice shook Rose's hand and gave her a hug of acceptance.

Father then said, 'Looks like we have to set up another place at the dinner table. '